# DEFYING GRAVITY

# DEFYING GRAVITY

## EARTH'S SECRET ALLIANCE

MARY GOSS: EPISODE 1

# TONY B. RICHARD

## WITH LYDIA PAYGE

Third Edition, October 2025

Illustrated by Hunter worth Sandra Illustrations © 2025 by Hunter worth Sandra. art rights reserved.
Interior designed & edited by Tigerpetal Press

ISBN 978-1-0698372-2-6 (paperback)
ISBN 978-1-7781914-8-0 (ebook)

visit *www.tonybrichard.com*

*Dedicated to my wife, Lydia, who has stood by my side through thick and thin. This book would not be possible without her.*

*Also dedicated to all people who persevere in the face of bullying, and those who are different in any way. Know that you are loved.*

# TABLE OF CONTENTS

| | | |
|---|---|---|
| 1 | A Man's World | 1 |
| 2 | The Interview | 14 |
| 3 | One Small Step for Mary | 21 |
| 4 | The Best Yet | 27 |
| 5 | A Kindred Spirit | 41 |
| 6 | The Weight of Gravity | 55 |
| 7 | Retrospection | 68 |
| 8 | The Prototype | 82 |
| 9 | The Launch | 87 |
| 10 | The Rescue | 96 |
| 11 | Humble Pie | 109 |
| 12 | An Unexpected Proposal | 115 |

| | |
|---|---|
| Did You Enjoy This Book? | 121 |
| Acknowledgments | 123 |
| Pronunciations | 124 |
| Series Timeline | 125 |
| About the Author | 128 |

# CHAPTER ONE

# A MAN'S WORLD

*October 1947*

"*We have reached the moon, sir,*" the pilot's voice crackled over the radio. "*Nuclear torpedo ready to launch. Destination distance, five miles.*"

The general's face was a neutral mask. His hawkish eyes were sharp and his lips were set into a firm line. "Launch."

"*Roger.*"

A loud whooshing filled the audio. A second later, the torpedo appeared on screen, flying out into the depths of space. The image on the monitors burst into light, and then the screens fizzled and went black.

"What happened?" the general demanded. "Get me eyes on them, *stat!*"

Mary's fingers flew over the keyboard so fast they almost blurred. A nearby probe brought itself around to the spacecraft's last location. New images were projected on the high-tech screens: One showed the moon, vast, cold, and empty. Next to it, suspended in space, was the spacecraft. It was completely dark.

"I've found them," she informed the others, "but they are on a collision course toward the moon. I estimate that they have about two hours before they crash."

The general looked down at Mary. "Doctor, it sounds like you have two hours to save their lives. I suggest you get on with it."

*Six Months Earlier*

BOSTON, MASSACHUSETTS

The door seemed more foreboding than any other time she'd stood in front of it, but Mary still pushed herself to knock. It was about time for the results of her dissertation to be ready, and she was certain it was the reason Professor Hunt had called her. Dread settled in her gut like a stone. If he wanted to see her personally, it probably wasn't good news.

"Come in," came the aged voice of her professor.

Mary pushed on the heavy wood door and entered. The smell of dust and stale pipe smoke overwhelmed her. The room hadn't changed since the last time she'd been there, with floor-to-ceiling shelves lined with thick books—many of which had been written by the man sitting behind the sturdy oak desk at the rear of the office. He thought he knew everything, but she proved him wrong several times.

When the professor saw Mary, his face dropped, and he groaned.

The professor huffed, and greeted her stiffly. She leaned over the desk to shake his hand, then he dropped hers, and she stepped back. His cold eyes stared at her over his long, thin nose. He'd been her mentor for all three years she had attended MIT and he hadn't changed one bit in all that time.

"You wanted to see me, Professor," she said, hoping to rid the air of its tension. Professor Hunt continued to stare at her, frowning.

"Yes," he said through his teeth. Slim fingers plucked a folder from amid the stacks of paper on his desk.

"This is the letter regarding your dissertation. I know I could have mailed it, but with you being the youngest and first female astrophysics doctoral candidate, I wanted to give it to you in person. You can now add a Ph.D. to your name. Of course, it won't be official until the June ceremony, but…congratulations, Dr. Mary Goss." The corner of his lip curled downward at the words, but Mary couldn't bring herself to care. She was smiling widely.

"Thank you, sir." She took the folder, flipping it open to marvel at her letter. "I was wondering if we could discuss sponsorship for my post-doctoral research?"

"I'm afraid I'll have to decline. We have brought you to this point in your journey, but neither I nor any other professor here can take you any further in your education or career. You have made it abundantly clear that you know far more than we do, and quite frankly, we're done hearing it. We will see you in June at the ceremony. Good luck, Dr. Goss." His accent was a hint more British than Bostonian.

He gave a dismissive wave of his hand, and then he returned to his work, as if she wasn't even in the room. Mary's fingers tightened around her letter. Head bowed, she headed to the door, but when she was about to turn the handle, she stopped. This was the last time she could vent to the professor. She took a deep breath. She couldn't contain her anger anymore.

"Excuse me, sir. You talk about how you and the other professors have had so much trouble teaching me, but what about the trouble I've gone through getting here? I'm labeled a genius regahding my knowledge, but I never had the chance to learn social skills." Mary's Boston accent was in full force.

"I spent a day in kindergahten, and the teacher called my ma to say she didn't know what to do with me because I already knew more than they teach at that age. The next day I was in grade one, and the same thing happened. By the end of the week, I found myself, still five years old, in grade three with a bunch of students who were eight and nine." Mary had to pause a moment, feeling the pipe smoke choking her.

"I spent the next two years in grades five and seven, attending middle school at eight. I spent two years there. The other students resented me because I was so much younger than them and so much smahtah. I tried to dumb down, but it just wasn't me." Looking at his face, she could see it was useless, but she just had to carry on.

"My parents knew it was tough, but they were too busy with their own teaching caheers to be able to help. I was transferred from my mom's science class because they thought we were cheating. I finally graduated high school when I was eleven and wore a junior bridesmaid dress to the prom because it was the only thing fancy enough that fit me." He opened his mouth, but Mary continued before he could speak.

"I stahted college the same year, and at first, I didn't have a clue what I was doing. It was so different from high school. I had to be responsible for my own supplies, books, and registering for classes. Some people did help me, but most just laughed at my expense. It was the first time I really felt stupid, so I vowed I'd never feel that way again.

"I worked hahd at my classes and got through my bachelor's degree in two years instead of four. Then my masters was equally fast, though certainly not easy." Mary gazed at the ceiling for a second.

"That brings me here. I came to you when I was sixteen, saying I wanted to get my doctorate in astrophysics. You were nice enough but you laughed as I walked out the door. Like before, I was determined to prove you and everyone else wrong, that I *did* belong and I *could* do it. So I researched more, read longer, and studied hahder than any of the other students. I came up with theories that you tore down and found known facts that went against your teachings." Mary looked directly at Hunt.

"Now, I know this won't change your mind about me, but it sure made me feel better getting it out."

Professor Hunt was sitting behind his desk with his lips pressed so firmly together that they were stark white. Mary couldn't tell if he was more shocked by her words or that she had the gall to say them. She decided it didn't matter and strode out the door, closing it for the very last time.

A little further down the hallway, Mary collapsed against the wall with a heavy sigh. Opening the folder again, she let her eyes scan it. The letter spoke of congratulations and praise, but she could read the contempt behind the words. *Why can't I get any respect in this place? It says here that I got high praise from the external examiners, but everyone treats me like a leper.* She pushed off the wall and headed outside.

"Hey! Look who it is!"

Mary looked up to see two students walking up the green. One of them was the tall and lanky figure of Chris Smith, a young man she knew well. He and his companion strode right up to her, and he swung an arm around her shoulders irreverently.

"If it isn't Miss Know-It-All herself. What weah you doing in there? Was Prawfessah Hunt just giving you the bad news that they don't give doctorates to gahls who think they'ah smahtah than Einstein?" His Boston accent was a little thicker than most of the students, as he was of Irish descent.

Mary rolled her eyes. *Why did I ever go out with this turkey? I'm glad it was only once.* She ducked her way out of his grip and walked away, feeling their eyes burning into her back and hearing Chris laughing as his friend whistled. She stiffened and told herself to ignore it, but before she could stop herself, she turned around and flashed them a smug grin. "That's *Doctor* Know-It-All to you."

GOSS FAMILY HOME

Mr. Goss was reading a paper in his living room chair when Mary entered. It had been a few months since Dr. Hunt gave her the letter—a few months since she'd left campus and never returned.

"How did the interview go?" her father asked.

She frowned. "Same as the others. Did you ask your friends what they said in my references?"

He looked over his glasses. "First, your professors ah not my friends. They ah from a different discipline. Second, when I do see them, they make some excuse and leave." Like Mary, his accent was very light, as they tried to avoid it on the university grounds.

Mary walked up to read the headline on the back of his newspaper. "Now they ah saying it's a weather balloon?"

Mr. Goss looked at the front page. "That's much more likely than aliens. If you do the math…"

Mary interrupted. "…Yes, yes, I know. It would take several generations for a ship to travel between solar systems, or the power requirements would be astronomical to get anywhere near the speed of light."

Mr. Goss nodded and went back to reading his paper.

"But how much power is released when you split an atom?"

"Energy equals mass multiplied by the speed of light squared; you know that. But they'll never be able to control that much energy. It's not good for anything but a bomb."

"I'm still hoping for aliens," Mary said.

"…therefore, we ah unable to offer you a position at this time."

With a cry of frustration, Mary threw the letter down onto the kitchen table next to the dozen others she'd already received. "I don't get it, Craig! It's been four months of applying since receiving my doctorate, and I've been rejected by every single laboratory in the state! I graduated from MIT with a PhD in astrophysics at the age of nineteen! Why ah they not impressed by that? Why can't I get a job? I'm so desperate at this point that I even left a résumé at the *ahmy recruitment office*, of all places! You know how I hate the ahmy."

Her brother, who was younger by a year, was preparing his fifth cup of coffee that day, filling the air with its rich aroma. He looked at her with knowing eyes and slurped some of his drink. He took it with three teaspoons of sugar, the *heathen*. "It's because youh prawfessahs hate you."

"It's not my fault that theah ah obvious flaws in their teaching. What am I supposed to do? Just ignore their mistakes?" Mary stood up, the legs of her chair scraping against the tiles, and started pacing.

"That's exactly what you should've done, genius. It sure would make life easier for *me*."

Mary grumbled. "What ah you talking about?"

Craig took another gulp of coffee before putting his mug down on the counter. "Do you know what it's like to be the *great* Mary Goss's brawther? Half of the univahsity expects me taw be as smaht as you, and the awthah half just hates me because you'ah my sistah. If you'd just kept youh head down and gone through school without a fuss, I wouldn't have taw deal with that!"

Mary rolled her eyes. "That's not my fault either. They shouldn't be judging you for who youh family is."

"OK, fine, but listen, Mary. You know how much those old prawfessahs hate being questioned, let alone proven wrawng. It's even worse because you'ah the only gahl in youh field. And you wonder why you couldn't get any of them to spawnsah youh pawst-dawctoahal work, and why none of the labs will hiah you?"

"My prawfessahs probably gave me bad references. I sweah it feels like the whole world is against any person who is not a white male. Doors ah always closed for the rest of us."

Craig shrugged. "Like it oah nawt, that's the way the woahld works. You'll just have taw get used taw it."

"Sure, *you'd* say that. You fit the description!"

"As you would say, *that's nawt my fault.* I'd like taw see you try taw change the woahld all by youh lonesawme."

Mary was about to snap back with a retort, but at that very second, the phone rang. Craig glanced over at it, then looked back at Mary with a clear *I'm not going to answer it* look. Familiar tingles raced up her spine—the very same tingling sensation that she felt on the cusp of her biggest decisions. She ignored the feeling, huffed, and grabbed the phone receiver off the side table, answering it.

A male voice addressed her. "Is Dr. Mary Goss available, please?"

Upon hearing her title, Mary felt the invigorating tingles again. Unbidden, her lips curled into a smile. "Speaking."

"This is Sergeant Dow of the US Army. We received your impressive résumé, and we would like to schedule an interview."

"That's kind of you to say so, but the recruitment office told me that they weren't hiring scientists," Mary replied. "And I don't want to build bombs." Really, the only reason she'd left her résumé at the recruitment office in the first place was because she'd felt a strong urge to do so. The inexplicable urge had been nudging her to apply all summer, and she'd finally given in only a few days ago. She figured they wouldn't even call back. How wrong she was.

The man on the phone laughed. "Dr. Goss, I assure you, we do more than just build bombs."

Mary scowled, shoving down the elated feeling that rose once again at the use of her new title. "Sure. I bet they told that to Einstein, too."

"Our aim here is to save lives, not end them. Going by your résumé, you seem perfect for the position we have available. Are you interested?"

Mary paused, considering the offer. On one hand, she'd never imagined herself working for the US Army, but on the other, she really needed a job. *What do I do? What do I say?* She looked over at Craig, who was watching her with curious eyes. Something told her to take the leap.

"Dr. Goss?" Sgt. Dow prompted.

"Yes, sorry. Yes, I'm interested."

"Would you be able to fly to New Mexico to meet me for an interview?"

Mary nearly choked. "New Mexico? Where exactly in New Mexico?"

"I'm sorry, that's classified."

"Well, I'm sorry too, but I don't make a habit of flying away to unknown destinations."

Dow was quiet, and she could hear low mumbling over the line, meaning he was probably speaking to someone else. He spoke again after a minute. "How about I come to meet you tomorrow afternoon at the recruitment office?"

"I'd be alright with that," Mary replied.

"Great. I will have them call you with the details."

"OK, but I'm still not building bombs."

Dow chuckled. "You won't have to build any bombs, Dr. Goss. I'll make sure of it. Good day." Then he hung up.

The elated feeling was back once more, this time swelling in her chest like a helium balloon. Her head felt light and her heart was racing. *Did I just do that?* She couldn't believe it.

"So, what's the big news?" Craig asked, startling her out of her thoughts.

"That was Sergeant Dow from the US Ahmy. He saw my résumé and wants to set up an interview," Mary told him breathlessly.

Craig frowned. "What could the ahmy possibly want with you? Ahn't you an astrophysicist?"

"I don't know." Mary turned away from him. What *could* the army want with her? Her focus was in understanding the cosmos. How could that be of any use to them? "I really don't know."

# CHAPTER TWO

# THE INTERVIEW

ARMY RECRUITMENT OFFICE

Mary arrived at the recruitment center wearing a floral sundress, but she immediately felt out of place as she looked around at all the men in their fatigues or plain clothes. As she was led to a side room, she sensed their eyes following her. They either had a stupid large grin on their face or an open mouth. One guy even whistled. *What am I, a piece of meat?*

The room was just big enough for a table and two chairs. Initially, she was thankful for the half-glass wall separating her from the men. Her mind buzzed with the thought of being alone in a small room with a man she'd never met before, but she shooed the thought aside. Yes, the room was small, but the blinds were open.

Then, she kept getting the feeling that someone was staring at her. Several times, she turned to meet a man's eyes and they would quickly look away. She wondered if she should close the blinds, but then she also didn't want to be in a closed room with a man. Her mind kept going in circles. *Should I close the blinds or leave them open?*

As her eyes raked over the men in the building, she wondered if any of them were Sgt. Dow. She glanced at the clock next. 3:10. She was a bit early, but early was good, in her opinion.

Yet another man passed by and glanced in through the open door, and her fingers dug into the fabric across her lap. She wrinkled her nose at the smell wafting over her. *What do women see in these military guys, anyway?* They were nice to look at, but....

Tingles raced along her spine and she shot up straight in her chair. Her eyes darted back and forth, wondering what was causing it. She only got these tingles in certain situations—of the life-changing variety. She'd had them when she first decided to attend MIT, and again when she chose astrophysics as her major. The feeling continued as the door to the main entrance opened and a young black man, about her age, entered the building. He immediately caught Mary's attention as he confidently strode through the office. It was all Mary could do to contain her surprise when he joined her in the room and closed the door.

"Dr. Goss, I presume," he greeted her. "Thank you for coming. I'm Sergeant Malcolm Dow. We spoke on the phone yesterday."

Mary rose and smoothed down her dress, reaching forward to shake his hand. When she spoke, she carefully enunciated her words to tone down her accent. "Yes, I remember. It's nice to meet you in person." His grip was firm, but his eyes were kind; they were nothing like the stern eyes she was expecting of a military man.

Once they were each settled in their chairs, Dow pulled out a folder of papers and adjusted his glasses. The front sheet was her résumé. Though he'd opened the file and pulled out a pen, Dow didn't look down, instead, he met her eyes with a friendly smile.

"Our scientists are impressed by your diss...," he coughed, "...writing, so this is just the routine. Why don't we skip the boring questions and get right to it."

Mary held back a sigh of relief. "Great."

"I know it's mentioned in my papers, but can you explain to me in layman's terms, what your specialty in astrophysics is?"

"Theoretical physics. I wasn't sure at first what I wanted to focus on, but I've always been curious about unexplained natural phenomena. With this specialty, I use mathematical models and abstractions of physical objects and systems to not only explain but rationalize and predict these phenomena."

He twiddled the pen between his fingers. "What made you want to study science?"

"Let's just say I had a good feeling about it."

Dow's eyes seemed to spark with interest. "Oh?"

She fidgeted. "Oh, it's nothing really. Just...sometimes, when I'm about to make a big decision, I get an odd sensation telling me that I'm doing the right thing. Women's intuition, I suppose."

"I understand." He smiled and winked. "I see that you were a straight-A student, but did you find any work?"

Mary bit her lip anxiously. "I was unable to get any references from my professors. Despite my academic record, it's been difficult in such a male-driven area of expertise."

Dow's smile faded, and he looked her in the eye sympathetically. "I know what you mean."

She found herself staring into his eyes; it was like she could feel all the hurt he had been through. It was like she'd known him for years, but she didn't know how that was possible.

Dow blinked. "Anyway, I understand you're not currently employed, but is there anything you've been working on?"

Excitement shot through her, and she perked up, leaning forward in her seat. "There is *something* I've been pondering lately. The theory of relativity states that nothing can move faster than the speed of light, but that's not necessahily true. I mean, if two objects were moving towahd each other at just below the speed of light, wouldn't they appeah to be going twice the speed of light, relative to each other?"

She paused to let him ponder the words, barely even realizing that her accent had slipped through in her excitement. He didn't seem to grasp the full depth of what she was saying, but he nodded all the same.

Mary lifted one shoulder. "I suppose it doesn't break this law, as they only *appeah* to be traveling faster, but even when I was little, I wondered why light is the fastest unit of measure in the universe. Something has to be, but what determines that? Gravity. If we could somehow manipulate gravity...." She fell into murmurs, her mind whirring with all the possibilities, and was only broken out of her thoughts when Dow gave a genuine laugh. She looked up, cheeks flushed bright red.

"I can tell right away that you are the one we've been searching for," he said, eyes twinkling.

Relief flooded through her.

"So," he said, "do you believe space travel is possible?"

She was surprised by the sudden change of topic, but answered, "Yes, I do. I think we have the technology and intelligence to make that happen in the very neah future."

"What about aliens?" Dow pressed. "Do you believe in them? And if you do, do you think they would be friendly?"

Mary paused before answering; she didn't want to appear foolish. "It's mathematically improbable that life doesn't exist elsewhere. Theah ah sevahl theories.

"Some say that if there were aliens out there, they would let us know. Others ahgue that aliens wouldn't interfere with our natural development. Or maybe they're equal to us in their scientific advancement and haven't invented ways to travel deep space yet.

"Personally, I *do* believe that theah ah aliens out there, and I believe that if we ever met them, we'd be able to establish peaceful relations."

He smiled. "Well said. You passed. The job is yours if you want it."

"And what exactly am I signing up for?"

"We are looking for civilians to help us with a project, although I can't give you any more details at this time. It's top secret, so if you choose to work with us, you won't be able to tell anyone the details of your location or the nature of your work—not even family. You will be living on base with very few outings until the work is complete. Do you accept these terms?"

"Yes." Her answer was immediate, and she surprised not only Dow, but herself as well. *Did I just say that? I...don't normally jump into things this quickly, but my intuition is telling me that I can trust him. And...at least it's better than being jobless.*

Dow's smile brightened further. "Wonderful! I'll pick you up tomorrow at oh-eight hundred hours at the address you have listed here."

"Oh-eight hundred hours?" she asked.

"Eight AM. Will you be ready by then?"

Mary's mind flashed through a list of everything she'd need to bring; then she nodded.

"Here is the standard contract and non-disclosure agreement. On it you will find information like your room and board. Your salary would start at a modest $200 a month. You can read it over, and if you are still interested, you can sign it and give it to me tomorrow. If you will excuse me for a moment."

Dow left the room and came back moments later with a new military-issue duffel bag. "Please limit yourself to this one bag, which you may fill with your clothing and personal items. If you change your mind, you can still say no in the morning, and there will be no hard feelings. This life is not for everyone. I'm staying at the big hotel down the street; if you have any questions, you can call me there."

After their farewells, he stood and exited the room.

Mary watched him leave, her eyes following him all the way back to the main entrance. As the door closed behind him, she blushed and turned her head away, scolding herself for staring. Collecting the papers and the bag, she smiled down at them, giddy and unable to stop trembling. She had a job! As soon as she got home, she had some exciting news to tell her family.

# CHAPTER THREE

# ONE SMALL STEP FOR MARY

GOSS FAMILY HOME

When Mary arrived, her parents were already home from work. Her father was sitting in his armchair in the living room with a book open in his lap, and it sounded like her mother was in the kitchen preparing dinner.

"I've exciting news!" she called out as she slipped off her pumps and put them away.

Her mother smiled delightedly at her as she entered the room. She pulled Mary into a hug and pressed a kiss to her cheek. "You told us you weah going for an intahview tawday. Did you get the jawb?"

"Yes, I did! Sergeant Dow told me I'm a perfect fit for the position!"

Those words caused her father to look up from his book. He turned to her, a deep frown marring his face. "Sergeant?" he repeated. "You joined the ahmy?"

Mary frowned back at her dad. Ever since she had declared she was applying to MIT, he'd been a constant voice of disapproval in her ear. He loved her; she was sure, and she knew he wanted her to have a good, easy life, but there were still times when his overprotective nature grated on her. This was one of those times.

"Yes, Dad," she said, walking over to him and hugging him over the back of his armchair. "I couldn't find work in any labs, so I dropped off my résumé at the recruitment office. I'm going to be a civilian consultant on a top secret project, and I'm leaving tomorrow morning at eight, so I'd better get packing."

He grunted, but her mom captured her in another hug, holding her tightly despite Mary's struggles. "That's so wondahful, deah! See, I told you that you would find something."

"Where is it?"

"Dad, I told you, it's top secret," Mary said as she finally escaped her mom's hold.

"Do you even know?"

Mary sighed. "Not exactly, but I've got a good feeling about it. I trust him."

Her dad suddenly looked suspicious. "Him? You mean the sergeant who interviewed you?"

Mary pointedly refused to answer. He often got like this, and she found that the best way to deal with it was to not engage at all.

Of course, that was also the cue for her mom to immediately begin fretting. "You've nevah lived away from home befoah. Will you be alright awn youhr own?"

"I'm suah I'll be fine, Mom. I'm smaht, remember? I'll figure it out. Besides, I've also nevah had a real jawb befoah. This will be good for me."

"But how will you suahvive with all those men around? It's the ahmy, you know; theah won't be many gawls around for you taw talk taw."

"There weren't many girls at school either, Mom. Anyway, I've nevah had a problem with men befoah," Mary reassured her. "I'll probably be working with them, but I doubt it'll be any worse than the lab work I did at university. They're not interested in me, and I'm not interested in them."

Her mom returned to the kitchen to finish dinner, so Mary deemed her soothed and walked to the stairs to head up to her room.

Once alone, she set the duffel bag on her bed and threw open her wardrobe doors. She'd filled the bag halfway before doubt set in. *Should I've agreed so easily? I know nothing about Sergeant Dow, or my new job for that matter. On the phone he said I wouldn't be making bombs, but what if that was a lie? He didn't mention it at all during my interview. What if he changed his mind?*

The thoughts churned, making her feel sick to her stomach. She couldn't even consider the notion of anything she invented being used to hurt someone.

*He's lying, he's lying, he's lying.* Thoughts of everything that could go wrong nagged at her. Dropping one of her plainer dresses, she sat on the bed, chest cold. *Maybe I should stay home and try my luck with those labs again,* she thought, *but…he came all the way here to interview me. And I might not get another chance like this!*

It was a once-in-a-lifetime opportunity for her to take, and she felt deep in her soul that she needed to reach out and grab it with both hands. She settled on the decision, feeling determined, and then that tingling feeling along her arms and the back of her neck returned, bringing a smile to her face. It was the right choice; she knew it.

She picked up her plain dress again and folded it, adding it to the bag. What she'd already packed were mostly basics and necessities, but what else was she supposed to bring to wear on a military base? *I suppose I'll be working in a lab most of the time, so I'd better bring along some sturdy shoes and plain clothes for under a coat, or just some casual clothes for research and study.*

She picked through the dresses still hanging there, considering each of them. Making a split-second decision, she grabbed one of the better-looking Sunday dresses and tossed it on top. *Just in case.*

\* \* \*

"Neahly time, deah. Be ready," Mary's mother advised, as she sat down at the breakfast table with two plates of toast and a bowl of hard-boiled eggs.

Mary grabbed an egg and rolled it on the table to fracture its fragile shell. "I know, Maw."

She was set. Her duffel bag was already sitting near the entrance with her travel shoes and coat, and she was dressed comfortably. The papers she'd been given at the end of her interview—all signed—sat on the table next to her. The clock read twenty to eight, which should give her enough time to finish eating and clean up before Sgt. Dow was due to arrive.

Just as she was finishing the last of her toast, she could hear the sound of an automobile pulling up outside and glanced out the window. Seeing a jeep stopping in front of the house, she looked at the clock. "Eight AM, just as he said."

A crisp knock sounded on the door and Mary stood up, but her father was closer. He opened the door and, with his foreboding stature, stared down at the young man standing there.

"Sergeant Dow, I presume?" he asked, his voice revealing nothing.

Mary watched his head go up and down as he sized up the sergeant.

Dow offered his hand to the tall man. "Yes, sir. Nice to meet you. You must be the senior Dr. Goss. I am here to pick up Dr. Mary Goss and escort her to the military base."

Mary's father accepted the handshake, but upon pulling away, he crossed his arms. "What will she be doing, and when will she be back?"

"I cannot give any details about the project, as it's top secret, but as a civilian, Dr. Goss will be allowed to leave anytime. If she chooses to stay during the entirety of the project, we will be keeping her busy until at least Christmas.

"Here is my card. If you need to get in touch with her, I will relay any messages." Dow peered around her father at Mary. "Are you ready to go, Dr. Goss?"

"Yes, I am. One moment, please." She wiped away the last of the crumbs and kissed her mother on the cheek. At the entrance, she put on her shoes, and squeezed her father extra tight, then grabbed the papers and duffel bag as she stepped out the door. "Bye. I love you both."

# CHAPTER FOUR

# THE BEST YET

## IN TRANSIT

The jeep ride was quiet, and soon they were at a small airfield. The hangar was only big enough for about a dozen small planes, some of which seemed very fancy, but Sgt. Dow led her past the hangar over to a DC-3 transport plane, which she only recognized because it was in an issue of *Popular Science*. She'd never been on a plane before, but once inside, she decided it wasn't as comfy as she'd expected. Un-padded metal seats ran along the walls and had cross-chest seatbelts, and in the air was an odd mixture of cleaning solution and gasoline. After stowing her bag under her seat and struggling a bit with the belt, Mary buckled herself in.

"We're all ready," Dow called to the pilot. Moments later, the engine revved, and the plane began to move.

Mary glanced out the window nervously as they picked up speed. A loud rumbling filled her ears. "Is it supposed to be making that sound?"

"Yes. No need to worry, Dr. Goss. You're perfectly safe," Sgt. Dow assured her. "It's a bit loud now, but once we're in the air, you won't even notice it."

He was right. As soon as they'd reached cruising altitude, the engine noise lessened from a roar to a hum.

Dow turned to her. "I can tell you more about the project now. I couldn't with the others around; I'm sure you understand. Even the mere existence of this project must be kept under wraps *at all costs*."

"Of course."

"So, when I asked you if you believed in aliens, I was serious. Aliens exist, and they made contact with us just last month. We've been working with them at the base we're headed to."

Mary's eyes widened. "Really?" She studied him closely, trying to find any sign in his face that would tell her he was joking—that this was some big prank. There wasn't any. "Yes!" she cried out as she did a celebratory shimmy in her seat.

He flashed a smile before his face turned grim. "But, if this were to get out, there would be a mass panic."

"That sounds serious."

He nodded. "Exactly, which is why I'm glad you've been so patient with me. So, where would you like me to start?"

A thrilling sensation washed through her and she couldn't keep the excited grin off her face. What to ask first? Should she try to learn more about the project or who she was going to be working with? "Tell me about the aliens first. Who ah they? Where ah they from? And how did they get here?"

Dow sat back and hummed, as if sorting through his brain for a place to begin. Mary wondered if this was because he knew so much about the aliens, or not enough. Perhaps there were things he could share with her, and things she couldn't know. She surely hoped to know all she could and waited with bated breath.

"They come from the planet Zalma, so we've been calling them the Zalmen. They came here to Earth in need of our help. The people from the planet Moad have been attacking them. The Zalmen's technology is leagues beyond ours, but they're pacifists, so they're at a severe disadvantage in the war."

Her elation quickly took a nosedive. "You promised I wouldn't have to build any bombs, but it sounds to me like I'm going to be building weapons for you anyway," she accused.

The sergeant immediately began waving his hands, eyes wide. "Oh, no, no, no. We don't want you to be making weapons, nor do we want to fight the invaders. As I said, the Zalmen are pacifists, and want us to resolve this through peaceful means. In fact, the Zalmen's primary purpose for coming here was to find a negotiator."

"That's a relief. I was worrying about it all night, but my intuition has never been wrong before." She paused, confused. "But if they needed a negotiator, why would you be looking for scientists? You'd think that you'd start with, well...*negotiators.*"

"Oh, we have," Dow assured her. "Don't worry. The head of this project, General Jones, brought in Ambassador Wilcox to negotiate the terms of our treaty with the Zalmen, and then negotiate with the Moadites. In exchange for our help, the Zalmen will provide us with their technology, which is highly advanced. Hence the need for genius scientists such as yourself."

Mary stiffened, unsure how to take the compliment. When she became aware of her cheeks heating, she quickly looked away. "I see," she said, "so this job will mainly be me leahning from the aliens. When do I get to meet them?"

"I'll personally introduce you when we get to the current base."

"And where's that?"

"Quite honestly? In the middle of nowhere. All the bases are, and we move quite frequently, so keep that in mind." He winked when Mary's mouth dropped open. Then he amended, "The location of the base is indeed classified, but I could have just as easily told you that it is in the middle of the desert, with nothing around for miles and with no official name. We call it Area 6."

\* \* \*

After a bumpy four-hour flight, they touched down. *This really is the middle of nowhere,* Mary thought to herself as she disembarked the plane behind Sgt. Dow. The hot, dry air hit her like the blast from a furnace. She looked around at the base, which was a collection of tents and other temporary buildings. Beyond the tents, barren desert stretched out as far as the eye could see, nothing but dusty shrubs for miles. Way off in the distance, she thought she could see some trees, but it would probably take a whole day of walking to reach them.

Dow directed her to one of the tents, and inside, she found three people standing around in reflective foil suits. She deduced that they must be the aliens, since even though they looked entirely human, one had green skin, another blue, and the third light purple.

Mary approached the blue alien, a young man with cropped black hair. She was tempted to touch the fabric of his suit, but refrained. Instead, she asked, "What kind of propulsion system do you use? Do you believe that there would be a way to influence the curvature of space and therefore decrease the force gravity inflicts on an object, thereby allowing that object to move at unforeseen speeds?"

The blue alien gaped at her. "U-um...," he stuttered.

Mary stepped back, disappointed. For all that Dow had been building up their advancements in technology, they weren't very well spoken, nor did they seem anything but baffled at her words. "I thought you said that the aliens were highly advanced?" she said, looking at the sergeant.

"I did," he agreed, as he tried to hide an amused smile. "Sorry, these aren't the *real* aliens. They're just army soldiers with painted faces, meant as a test for new recruits. It became protocol after one of our previous recruits saw a real alien and...went cuckoo; we had to sedate him. I'll take you to the Zalmen soon, but first, the general wants to meet you."

Mary puckered her lips. "General Jones? The one you mentioned on the plane?"

"No. General Jones recently left with a team and most of the aliens, back to their home planet. General Newman is in charge while he's gone." With a gesture for her to follow, he left the tent.

He took her to a different tent. Inside and seated behind a desk was a man in his mid-forties. Mary didn't know much about the army, but even she knew that he was surprisingly young for his position.

Dow stiffened and saluted, looking every bit the military man that he was. "General Newman, sir."

"I see you have been successful."

"Yes, I have, sir. May I present to you Dr. Mary Goss." He gestured, and Gen. Newman turned his attention toward her.

Internally, Mary panicked. *Do I salute too?* After a moment of hesitation, she attempted to copy Dow's salute. The general laughed as he stood up.

"At ease," he said.

Both Mary and Dow relaxed.

"Dr. Goss," the general continued, "I have heard a lot about you. I'm very pleased you joined the team."

Mary's pulse quickened. *Really?* What exactly had he heard? "Thank you...sir?"

"As you are a civilian, you don't need to salute or address me formally. But I *do* appreciate the occasional 'sir' when in the company of my men. Reminds them who's in charge." He nodded his head toward Dow and winked at her. Mary smiled back.

*He seems nice enough. Certainly not what I was expecting.*

Newman then pulled a metallic object from his pocket and offered it to her. It was small and flat, like an identification card or a pack of gum. "This is a Zalma communicator. Sergeant Dow or one of the Zalmen can show you how to use it if you like, but from what I hear, you're intelligent enough to figure it out on your own."

Mary accepted the object and immediately marveled at it, turning it over in her hands. *It's so sleek! I don't even see any seams.*

"Thank you, sir," she said, putting it away with all intent to study it in detail later.

"I'm sure Dow has filled you in on your job duties while you're here, but I want to be thorough. You will be attending instructional classes led by the Zalmen to learn about their technology. These classes are non-negotiable. Am I clear?"

Mary nodded sharply. "Crystal clear, sir. I can't wait to begin."

Newman cracked a smile. "Good. We're still in the early stages, so the main focus is for you to understand the technology and how to apply it to existing Earthly technology such as transportation and weaponry."

"Sir, if I may interrupt, I told Sergeant Dow that I refuse to make weapons. That was a condition of my employment. I will be happy to leahn, and happy to make innovations for transportation or otherwise, but I will *not* make anything that can be directly used to hahm anyone."

Newman snapped an angry look at Dow. Mary was surprised that Dow was able to look so calm in front of the angry general.

"Yes, sir. With all due respect, we are looking for a peaceful solution, right?"

Newman returned his stare to Mary, who took an unconscious step back. Her whole body was tense. She was a civilian, sure, but even *she* knew that it was rude to interrupt a general, let alone to contradict one. She would surely die of embarrassment if they sent her home on the first day of the job with her tail between her legs.

Then the general paused. His lips moved as if he'd already chosen his words and was testing to see how they tasted. He calmed, but his words were still stern when he spoke. "Very well, but you will be under the watch of the senior scientists. They will be the ones determining the projects. You'll have to take it up with them."

Mary breathed a sigh of relief. "Thank you, sir."

"That will be all." He looked away from her to Dow. "You may proceed. Dismissed."

As soon as they were outside and out of earshot Mary said, "That was horrifying."

Dow regarded her with his once-again unreadable expression. "I could tell. I've never seen anyone speak so strongly against a general before. You were brave to put your foot down." He huffed out a laugh. "Not that it's a good idea to speak to a superior like that, but…."

"Yeah…." Mary agreed. "I guess I thought I was talking to one of my professors."

Dow chuckled.

He led her to a third tent, the largest so far. The inside was set up like a schoolroom. Though there were tables and chairs, they were unlike anything Mary had seen before, hovering above the floor. There were a few blackboards—or what appeared to be blackboards, they were more silver—scattered about. At the front of the room was a vehicle resembling a futuristic van, made of smooth, reflective metal. It had wraparound windows, was devoid of tires, and was hovering, much like the tables and chairs were. There was one lady and two children in the room.

They were all bald and wearing foil robes similar to the fake aliens. The lady's skin was the color of a fern, and she was writing on one of the boards with a finger. As Mary drew closer, the alien turned.

"Dr. Goss, I would like you to meet Sarara. She will be one of your teachers," Dow introduced.

Mary eyed the woman cautiously. "Ah you real? Or ah you another test?"

The woman, Sarara, looked alarmed for a moment, and her green skin flashed red, green, then blue in rapid succession before returning to fern. "Are you referring to the men that they have painted different colors? Yes, I am real."

"You also change color? How do you do that?" Mary couldn't help asking. Then, upon seeing Sarara's stricken expression, she backtracked. "Oh, I'm so sorry! That was rude of me."

"It's OK, we get asked that a lot," the young girl said.

"These are my two children, Janara and Takar," Sarara said.

"We heard that you are the smartest human on Earth," Takar said with a smile.

"I don't know about that," Mary said.

Dow excused himself after that, citing many more things he had to do. He bid them good day and said he might see them later in the mess hall for dinner.

Sarara nodded to Dow, then signaled Mary to follow her. They settled at one of the tables, with the two children sitting close. Sarara was quick to begin. "My people and I come from Zalma, a planet in the star system you call Tau Ceti."

"It is approximately twelve of your light-years from here," Janara added.

"Twelve light-yeahs? Did it take you that long to get here?"

"No. Our ships can travel at much faster speeds," Sarara said.

Mary leaned forward. She couldn't believe it. Something she'd only just theorized—and argued at length with her professors about—was already a reality. "You can travel faster than the speed of light? That's amazing! How long was the trip?"

"Five months," Janara said with a smirk.

Mary was rendered speechless. Then, ever so slowly, a smile spread across her face. "I am so excited to be working with you. Where do we staht?"

"Staht?" Takar asked.

"Start." Janara rolled her eyes at her brother. "I understood it."

"Takar, remember, people on Earth speak different languages and have different...accents, I believe?" Sarara asked.

Mary nodded. "I come from a place called Boston. People tell me we tend to miss a lot of Rs and slur our Os." She made sure to pronounce it properly. She made a mental note to control her accent.

"Now, go back to your homework, and next time be more polite." Sarara shook her head.

Mary and Sarara spoke straight through until dinner. They walked together with the children to the mess hall, still deep in conversation. Entering the tent, they saw Dow, Newman and another sergeant (which she recognized by his uniform) sitting together at a table with a green-blue alien.

As Mary had found out, all of the Zalmen were bald, and their base color corresponded to their character. Sarara had been hesitant to reveal that, explaining that it was a deeply personal aspect of her species, so when she finished, Mary didn't press, though she knew the other woman had more to say.

The blue-green alien joined them as they headed up to the front to wait in line, and Sarara introduced him to Mary as her husband, Kanara, who was an engineer. He was "quite brilliant" according to Sarara, and he complimented his wife in turn, saying that she was one of Zalma's brightest scientists, which caused Sarara's skin to blush furiously magenta.

"Oh, brother...." Takar looked at Mary with a wink and a smile. "Did I say it right?"

Mary couldn't answer, but nodded as she laughed.

Once receiving their vegetarian meals, they joined the sergeants and general, and Sarara immediately turned to Dow.

"Where did you find Mary—um—Dr. Goss? She is the best you have brought to me yet!"

Mary, not expecting the compliment, blushed. "I'm just glad to finally have a teacher who knows what she's talking about. I've never had such stimulating discussions!"

Mary sat between Sarara and Dow. The conversation was mostly small talk, scattered with questions. Sarara and Kanara discussed projects and new discoveries. Their children asked Mary a dozen questions.

On Mary's other side, Newman, Dow and the other sergeant—Rabinowitz—were locked in a conversation about Gen. Jones and his team and the latest update of their journey into space. Mary split her attention, listening to both, occasionally chiming in with her own thoughts, but she mainly observed. It was all very fascinating.

"How are things going for you in the engineering laboratory?" Sarara asked. "Those men of yours don't seem to want to cooperate."

Kanara sighed. "It is going as well as it can be. Some of the engineers are refusing to heed my advice and teachings. They are prideful; they wish to succeed without my aid."

"I see. Humans are strange creatures that way." She looked over at Mary apologetically, then asked, "Mary, do you know any methods we may use to remove this obstacle?"

"No, sorry. That's pretty much how all the men I've worked with ah like. They need to prove that they ah the best. They won't accept help, much less from a woman." She shrugged. "I don't mind, though. I'm much smahtah than most of them, anyway." Embarrassment washed over her again as she heard her own accent.

Concern flashed across Sarara's face.

"If you don't mind me asking, what ah*re* you working on?" Mary tried to compensate for her accent.

Kanara, having finished his meal—a bun and some peculiar-looking steamed vegetables—pushed his plate away and turned to her. "The human engineers are building a new spacecraft, but there is not much to report thus far. I am helping with the technological components. If you wish to visit, I would be happy to show you around."

# CHAPTER FIVE

# A KINDRED SPIRIT

Earth–Zalma Basecamp, Arizona

When Mary returned from breakfast with Sarara and Kanara, she found four men sitting in the back rows of the classroom. Two other men were standing near the front, and Sarara introduced them. "Mr. Lance Harper and Mr. Randy Quinn, this is Dr. Mary Goss."

Mary raised her hand to shake.

Quinn was of average build, with copper-toned hair and brown eyes. He hunched a little and looked at Mary with curiosity. "Hi-hi," he said, starting to extend his own hand.

Harper let out an incredulous scoff, causing Quinn to jump and quickly drop his hand. Harper was exceptionally tall, with ash-blond hair and blue eyes. His build told Mary that he exercised regularly, but he didn't stand straight enough to be a soldier.

"*Doctor?* This girl? She's a teenager. What could she possibly be a doctor of? The kitchen?"

"The culinary ahrts have chefs, not doctors," Mary corrected snidely. She had a harder time controlling her accent when angry and already knew that she wouldn't like this man one bit.

Harper flashed his teeth in a sharp grin. "Oh… I'm sorry, doll; I didn't know we had a scholar on the team."

"At least I *am* a scholar. What's your education? Kindergarten? And don't call me doll!"

His face flushed red, and at his sides, his hands were clenched into fists.

Quinn's eyes went wide and darted between the two of them. His own hands made an aborted movement like he wanted to intervene but wasn't sure how. He touched Harper's shoulder, but was roughly brushed aside.

"I will *not* be spoken down to by a *girl*," Harper said forcefully. "I'm the chief engineer here. I'm the one in charge! You—will—listen—to—me."

Mary was about to retort, but Sarara cut in before she could. "That is correct. Mr. Harper holds the position of highest seniority and is therefore the one who leads this project. Now that introductions are complete, let us all sit down and begin today's lesson."

She stepped between them and gestured for them to sit. Mary glared, while Harper sent her a look like the cat that ate the canary. As he and Quinn returned to the middle row, Mary sat in the front. She couldn't see anyone else in the room aside from Sarara and Kanara, and while this method had worked in her favor in university, it was working against her here.

Harper was a big man, not like the geeks in school. For the first time in her life, she felt physically threatened. His hot breath reeked. He was close enough to hit her. She wanted to move but didn't want to give him the satisfaction.

"General Jones believes the Moad reverse-engineered the Zalma probe they captured. Luckily for us, the technology in it was basic. It had a sub-light-speed nuclear drive, navigation computer, audio and video transmitters, but no deflectors.

"The drive used a controlled nuclear reaction to propel it, unlike our anti-gravity drive, which allows us to modify gravity. This, in turn, allows us to travel faster than light—"

"This is ridiculous!" Harper said, speaking over her. "You can't change gravity; it's a constant. And Einstein's theory of relativity proves that you can't go faster than light."

Sarara changed multiple colors. "That is not correct, Mr. Harper. Modifying gravity is indeed possible. My people have been doing it for a century, and we did it to get here."

Mary glanced over her shoulder to see Harper leaning back in his chair, looking skeptical. Some of the other men were rolling their eyes. Quinn was the only one who seemed interested, but after one look from Harper, he ducked his head.

Mary frowned. "What's wrong with you? Sarara and Kanara are living proof. Science is being rewritten every day as new discoveries ah being made and hypotheses tested." Her cheeks burned as she saw Harper's reaction to her accent.

Harper laughed snidely. "*Ah* being tested," he said in a high-pitched voice, mocking her.

Turning back to the front, Mary saw that Sarara's skin was still flickering between various colors, which she understood as discomfort. After watching her interaction with Kanara the night before, Mary couldn't blame her. Clearly, she wasn't used to this kind of bigotry. Nor the blatant ignorance. Mary wasn't going to let it stand.

"And gravity is not a constant," Mary said, twisting around in her seat again. "It is determined by the curvature of space. Being able to modify that curvature would allow the Zalmen to manipulate the relation between space and time, and therefore travel faster than the speed of light." Mary's anger exploded as she defended her new friend. "She's not saying that Einstein's theory is wrong, just that it can be updated as new information arises. That's why it's called a *theory*."

Harper stared at her blankly for a split second before letting his face fall into one of complete rage. The men behind him remained stuck in confusion, blinking wide eyes and looking like lost puppies.

"How long do we have to sit here and listen to you dames talk nonsense? It was bad enough with just the alien. Now we have a brainiac Kewpie doll adding her two cents. Well, I for one have had enough of the both of you and your science fiction. I live in the world of science *fact*. Let's just go work on our ship." He got up, and the other men followed suit, but Quinn hesitated. He was looking at Mary with another inquisitive expression, dark eyes locked on her. Harper noticed. "Come on, Quinn! Move it!"

The moment was broken, and Quinn scurried after Harper and the others.

Kanara sighed and turned to Sarara. Neither spoke, but an understanding seemed to pass between them as they both turned blue. Mary wondered if they were talking telepathically. Then Kanara pressed his forehead to Sarara's briefly, and they returned to their normal colors. Sarara and Mary watched Kanara as he followed the men out of the room.

"That works out pleasantly for us," Sarara said once he was gone. "Now we can converse uninterrupted. Kanara will work with them on the nuclear drive; it's simple enough for them to understand. Why don't we work on something more modern? *Computer, switch to Gravity Drive lesson.*

"The anti-gravity drive is comprised of several components, the first of which being the outermost structure, our vacuum capsule," Sarara continued, and Mary leaned forward, grinning eagerly.

Mary closed her notebook. Her arm was sore from all the writing she had done, but it was a good ache, and she was pleased with the progress they'd made. She'd filled pages upon pages with complex mathematics and even added her own observations and questions in the margins. Glancing at her wristwatch, she noted that they still had half an hour of scheduled class time, even though they'd flown through the first lesson and moved onto the next.

"How did I do for my first lesson?" Sarara asked. "I have never completed one so swiftly before, not even on Zalma." Sarara turned a different shade of green for a moment. "And with these men, I must normally repeat myself several times, and they still don't understand."

Mary laughed. "Ah you saying that I'm the best student you've evah had?"

"Without a doubt," Sarara agreed. She didn't seem to understand Mary's wisecrack, but Mary didn't correct her.

"Wow. Since we have extra time before dinner, there's something I've been meaning to ask you."

Sarara summoned one of the hover chairs and sat across from Mary. She seemed to be expecting a question concerning the class, but Mary had already closed her notebook and put it aside. Instead, Mary took out her communicator and set it between them.

"Your communicators. General Newman gave me one, but he didn't tell me how it worked. I've already discovered that it responds to voice commands, but I doubt it could tell me anything about how it was built. I was hoping you could fill in the gaps."

"Certainly. We call these devices communicators, but it is also a very powerful quantum calculating machine, which we call a computer; you may have heard me using the term earlier. It can do any computation in a fraction of a second."

"Quantum, as in quantum physics, sub-atomic?"
Sarara nodded.

"Wow! So, it's not just a telephone. How would that work?"

"Voice commands. You merely ask it a question, perhaps *Communicator, calculate the time for a flight to the moon at half the speed of light.*"

"*Approximately two-point-six-six seconds,*" came a disembodied female voice.

Mary jumped and looked around. "Who said that?"

Sarara blushed. "Oh, I apologize. Unlike your hand-held device, my communicator is woven directly into my clothing."

"In your clothing? Is that why it's foil?"

"Yes."

"Amazing! How does such a small device work so quickly and have such information in it?"

"The device is comprised of a nearly infinite number of microscopic robots called *nanites* that network to solve any task or question that you ask of it," Sarara explained. "And, should it not have the information you require, it will connect with other communicators."

Mary frowned. "Infinite?"

"Not quite infinite," Sarara clarified, "but the number is so large that I do not believe you humans have a name for it."

"Wow!" Mary was astounded.

"Speaking of communication, I was not aware you were given your communicator already. Everything I write on my boards is accessible through your communicator, as well as these tables, for that matter."

"These tables are communicators too?" Mary's eyes raked over the tiny device in her hand and the large one she was sitting at. They were unassuming; no one would expect that it was capable of such feats.

*That must be why there are no seams!* However, there was still one thing left unanswered. "How did you develop such tiny robots?"

Sarara's lips curled into a smile. "That is an excellent question for a future lesson."

*A couple nights later*

"Dr. Goss! Wake up!"

Mary jolted awake in her tent, and her first thought was that she'd slept in. That couldn't be right, though, as she realized that it was Sgt. Dow speaking from outside her tent. He wouldn't be the one sent to wake her up. Furthermore, her tent was dark, meaning that it was still night outside. Yet she heard army boots crunching on the dry dirt and automobiles moving.

There was another call from outside, so she quickly got out of bed and pulled a housecoat on over her nightgown. She peeked out of the tent. As expected, it was Dow. Behind him, soldiers were running back and forth, packing up tents and loading up trucks.

"What's going on?"

"An unknown aircraft was sighted flying overhead. We don't know if it's an enemy or not, but our location could be compromised. Our next move was scheduled for the morning, but General Newman thought it best that we leave immediately," he told her.

"OK…. Just give me a minute to dress and throw my things together."

"Alright. We're loading the trucks now. Departure is in fifteen minutes."

He left, and Mary ducked back into her tent. In record time, she'd changed into a clean blouse and skirt, and she was stuffing everything else into her duffle bag. It wasn't as neat as the first time she'd packed, so she had to force the zipper closed. As soon as she came out with her bag, she was ushered into one of the trucks by a soldier. Several more leaped into the action of disassembling her tent.

She was seated between two large men. They were both sitting with their legs spread wide and, with her bag on her lap, the space felt even smaller. It was even worse than the time her family had gone on a road trip when she was young and had been squished between walls of luggage.

The next indeterminate stretch of time was the most boring and most uncomfortable of her life thus far. The men had obviously helped with the packing, as they were sweaty and extremely warm. The air was stuffy, and despite the smell, she was fighting not to fall asleep on one or both of the men's shoulders. Every time she came close, she would think to herself, *That would be humiliating!* which was an excellent deterrent. At some point, she remembered she could access her class notes on her communicator and pulled it out, hoping to at least stimulate her mind. It worked for the most part.

Then the truck stopped, and Mary stumbled out, finding that the landscape hadn't changed much. Still, it must have been far enough away because the men began unpacking and setting up the tents and other temporary buildings. Mary wobbled, well on her way to falling asleep on her feet.

By the time Dow approached her, she'd made it beyond exhaustion and back to wakefulness.

"Sorry about the move. There is another general trying to find us. We think he's still loyal to the president, but believes that the aliens are a threat, and wants to kill them all. Luckily, he's in a Canadian jail, but his people are still obeying his standing orders and are getting closer and closer to us every day."

"How did he end up in Canada if he's been tailing you down here in the south?"

"Funny story. Maybe I'll tell it to you sometime."

"Way to hold me in suspense," Mary teased. It came out more playful than she'd meant it to; she blamed it on her lack of sleep.

"Fine," Dow said, heaving an equally playful sigh. "Long story short, General Scornson tried to track us with a bugged briefcase, but my communicator intercepted the signal and sent him on a wild goose chase. Canadian goose chase, that is." He grinned, which Mary couldn't help but mirror.

"You should get some rest before the sun comes up."

Mary shook her head. "Can't. I'm up now, and I know I won't be able to get to sleep. I'm going to find Sarara and see if she's available. See you later."

* * *

"…and that ends today's lesson," Sarara said.

"Thanks. Have you come up with any ideas on how to move the tents with the anti-gravity drive?" Mary asked.

"As I said before, it is not just a matter of making a smaller version. Some of the components are too small already."

"Yes, you said that before, but have you had any inspiration?"

Sarara's skin turned white. "Inspiration?"

"Yes, any creative thoughts?"

Sarara's skin turned many colors. "I am afraid that my people do not have creativity. We only learned about it when we arrived here on Earth. You humans have creativity to spare. We love your art, literature, music, and more. You even have found creative ways to use our technology."

Mary shook her head. "What do you mean, your people don't have creativity? It's a necessity for advancement. Without imagination, you severely limit your problem-solving skills. Technology is born from solving problems. There is no way your technology could be so advanced if none of you has ever had an original idea."

"Have you had any creative ideas?" Sarara smirked.

"I was wondering…what if we only reduced the vacuum tube to ten percent instead of five?"

"Let us run that through the computer and see."

Later, when Mary lay in bed ready to fall asleep, she realized that she'd never gotten her answer.

After a few days at their newest base, Harper interrupted one of Mary and Sarara's lessons.

"What ah you doing here?" Mary sneered.

"As head of this department, I need to check in on everyone—including you two. What are you working on?"

"You wouldn't understand if we told you," Mary said.

"I have to approve any and all projects, so if you're doing any of that gravity bending, you can stop right now. The main focus of this department is getting my ship ready for its test flight. Do you have anything to offer?"

Mary's fingers tightened into fists, but she held her head high. "You may be my superior in this department, but you will never match my knowledge or ability." She couldn't help herself. He'd just come in to rub his authority in her face and she wouldn't stand for it. Ignoring Sarara's warning look, Mary rose from her seat and stood eye to eye with Harper—or as close as she could come with the height difference. "You might learn a thing or two if you stayed in Sarara's class, but you're afraid of anything new."

"Shows how much *you* know," Harper snarled, and with that, he stomped out of the room.

"It's been nice not having to deal with that every day," Mary said.

"It has been nice not having to repeat myself. In addition, I am enjoying your creative thoughts. It has resulted in very good discussions."

"And, oddly enough, I find it refreshing when you prove me wrong."

"It is not often when I find you wrong," Sarara said.

# CHAPTER SIX

# THE WEIGHT OF GRAVITY

## EARTH–ZALMA BASECAMP, ARIZONA

Mary and Sarara were working on the boards when Harper entered. "I hope you two are enjoying each other's company. What are you working on?"

"Improvements to your nuclear engine," Mary routinely answered.

"Good." Harper walked out.

Mary and Sarara laughed.

"These moves ah a pain. The last time we had to wait, because there were strangers in the area, and then we left tire tracks to boot. And now we ah moving twice a week," Mary said. "I wish we could get this miniature anti-gravity to work, but I'm a theorist, not an engineer."

"I suggest you ask Mr. Quinn," Sarara said. "Before you showed up, Mr. Quinn was the most committed and intelligent. He would be well suited to this project."

Mary grunted. "And how am I going to get his help? You heard Harper. He isn't going to approve any projects involving gravity. For that matter, he won't support anything I suggest."

"I do not know, but I believe you are letting your emotions get the better of your mind," Sarara said. "You must acknowledge that if you do not extend your hand to Quinn, he cannot extend his back to you."

"I've always been the one to *extend my hand,* as you say. For once, I'd like my peers to show me the respect that I've earned!"

"I have only been on your planet for two months, but I already know that your wishes are not possible. Your people are flawed. Males and females are separated, not only by rules and conventions, but by career choice.

"Any who strays from these roles are regarded with fear, and therefore, hostility. You must work not twice as hard, but three or four times if you wish to be held in high esteem by your peers. Quinn is the same. If you treat him with the same disdain as you treat Mr. Harper and the others, he will not come to you."

"I suppose you're right," Mary admitted. "You know, you're very good at giving advice for someone with no creativity. Maybe you do have imagination, but it is limited to personal interactions. I mean, my imagination is great when it comes to science, but limited when it comes to music and other arts."

"Interesting. So, there are different forms of imagination. I suppose that is why I could study your species for years upon years, and I would not be able to unravel how your mind is able to find creative uses for our technology, or make music, or write fiction."

More than giving great advice, Sarara was always able to make Mary smile. "I could study forever and not be able to speak as eloquently as you—especially in a second language. I guess that's one of the great mysteries of the universe. So, what will we be doing today?"

Quinn, as it turned out, was a hard man to find—or at least to get alone, as he was always with Harper. He tagged along everywhere the chief engineer went, whether it be working on the ship, eating in the mess hall, or sleeping in the barracks. Even worse, the four other men—two mechanics and two scientists—were usually with them.

Then, when Mary saw the six of them finishing up to head to the mess hall for dinner, the tingling sensation fluttered up her neck and over her shoulders, and she decided to take her chance. Quinn was lagging at the back of the group, so she hoped what she was about to do wouldn't cause a scene.

"Pssst!" she hissed quietly. When Quinn paused and looked at her, she motioned for him to come.

"Quinn!" Harper shouted. He hadn't noticed her. "What's with the holdup? Come on, or all the food will be cold!"

Quinn glanced at Mary, who gestured urgently again, sending him a pleading look.

"You...You go ahead," Quinn called out. "I'll catch up with you later, OK?"

Harper sent him a suspicious look. "What's with you?"

"I...I think I left the...ah...Autoclave on."

Harper stared at him a moment longer as if he was trying to pick apart Quinn's words for a lie. After a few seconds, either he saw no lie or just gave up—it didn't matter—because he shrugged. "Yeah, whatever." Harper left.

Quinn followed Mary back to the schoolroom.

"Hi-hi. What's up?" he asked suspiciously.

Mary fidgeted for the longest time, not looking at him. She rubbed her fingers together, drawing circles on the back of her hands, scratching at invisible itches. Finally, she looked up. "I feel like we might have got off on the wrong foot, so I want to apologize."

Quinn nodded.

"OK. I'm sorry for my behavior since I arrived. We haven't spoken much, but the times we have, I've been kind of rude. I know there is no excuse, but you must know that being one of the only women in my field has been an issue for me ever since I got into MIT."

Quinn's soft, steady eyes comforted Mary.

"No one ever takes me seriously because I'm a girl, so I'm sorry if I came across as blunt or hostile."

Quinn shrugged. "You mostly talked down to Harper, and no one likes him, but thanks for the apology. I have to admit; you really took me by surprise. I've never seen a lady like you before—talking about science, I mean. My sisters were never interested in anything I was learning in my physics and engineering classes. It's refreshing, but weird. You really seem to understand the science these aliens brought us."

Mary was struck by the words. That was the only way to describe the feeling welling up in her chest. Tears filled her eyes, and even though she fought against them, they fell. She quickly wiped them away. It wasn't much in the way of compliments, but she was half-expecting Quinn to just walk out after a few thinly veiled insults about her age or appearance. Guilt crept in. How could she have thought that?

"So, what's up?"

A shiver ran up her spine again. "Sarara has been teaching me about how they control gravity—you know that—but we've also been discussing how the invisibility technology works."

Quinn went pale. "Invisibility? They can make things invisible, too?"

"Oh, you didn't know that?"

"No, probably because Harper is not accepting their technology well, and he might go ballistic if he found out."

"That makes sense. But if we are successful, he will find out soon enough. The anti-gravity and invisibility use different frequencies of the same magnetic field; I want to incorporate them into one, so we can make almost everything in our mobile base become invisible and float to our new destination."

"So, we wouldn't be leaving tire tracks *and* we'd be invisible? That's great! But I would save the invisibility for emergencies; I don't think Harper could handle it."

Mary nodded. "Good point. We can build it, but I will have to ask General Newman not to use it unless it's absolutely necessary. Anyway, with your help, we'd be able to build the engine, then convert any vehicle and make remote modules for the tents so they can be towed as well." She looked him in the eye. "I am not an engineer, nor a mechanic. I can tell you how the physics works, but beyond that, I don't know what to do. Sarara said you were the one who understood the most before I came to class. Can you build it?"

The engineer paused and looked at the calculations that Mary had laid out. "Yes, I think we can do this. But we will have to do it without Harper's knowledge, which will be more of a challenge for me than you."

"I'll help any way I can," Mary promised. She couldn't wait to get started.

* * *

"Malcolm! Hello! It feels like forever since I've seen you." Mary wasn't sure exactly when she'd begun calling Sgt. Dow by his first name, but it had happened sometime in the past few weeks, and it just stuck.

Dow's face lit up as she sat at his table in the mess hall. "I suppose it has. I only ever make it to dinner on weekends, if at all. There's always something to do, plus the amount of time I spend traveling to find new recruits. It seems I never have a chance to sit and enjoy a meal. You know what I mean?"

"Definitely. I often eat in the classroom with Sarara and her family. Their Ambassador Geogram joins us frequently; he mentions you a lot."

"All good things, I hope?"

"He speaks very highly of you," she admitted. Then, teasingly, "Not sure what you've done to deserve it...."

Dow's mouth dropped open. He mimed doubling over in pain as if she'd shot him. "Ouch! Right in the weak spot!"

"Anyway," Mary continued, "I'm so excited to tell you about what I've been learning! Zalma science is so incredibly advanced; what they call fundamental physics is *centuries* beyond us." Mary beamed. "It's like

I'm learning the secrets of the universe, and we haven't even been into space yet."

"Really? That sounds exciting. Are you keeping up alright?"

Mary puffed out her chest. "Of course. Who do you take me for?" She smiled at him. "I mean, it helps that I'm the only one attending class, and Sarara and I have grown close. Even after she finishes the lesson, we keep talking about possible applications for the science.

"The only thing that bothers me is the computers—communicators. The Zalmen don't have any creativity, and yet they have all this advanced technology. Whenever I ask Sarara about it, she keeps dodging my questions."

Dow tilted his head thoughtfully. "You didn't meet Ambassador Wilcox, did you?"

"No. Why?"

"He's our Earth ambassador. He's actually on his way to Zalma with the team, but while he was negotiating the treaty between the Zalmen and us, Geogram let it slip that they were taught their technology by someone else. When Wilcox asked who, Geogram wouldn't answer."

Mary hummed to herself, perplexed. "Should we be concerned?"

"I don't think so; I have a good feeling about the Zalmen. A hunch, if you will."

"Just like my intuition!"

"Exactly. Oh, speaking of the ambassador, I hear that Miss Warren, Wilcox's assistant, designed new uniforms for us—all of us, including you civilians. The idea is everyone will feel more like a team. I hear that you would have a choice of a blouse or polo shirt and pants or a long or short skirt."

"I don't want to wear a uniform."

"It will be optional for civilians. So, what else have you been learning these past few weeks? I'd love to hear about it—even though most of it will probably fly right over my head."

"Quite literally, in most cases." Mary moved her hand over her head. "I'm learning about the anti-gravity drive that the Zalmen use to fly their ships. They manipulate gravity to fly, so Sarara and I have been getting into discussions about using gravity manipulation on a smaller scale."

"What do you mean?"

"Their deflectors work to reverse gravity to push objects, but normally gravity pulls. I was wondering if we can use that same technology in a handheld device. I'm still working out the mathematics, but it's got a good base, and Quinn has been a huge help in designing the prototype."

"Prototype? Sorry, I think you've lost me."

Mary grinned. "We're building a gravity gun."

"I thought you didn't want to design weapons," Dow pointed out.

"Well, 'gun' is a figure of speech. It's a nonlethal weapon, not meant to hurt anyone. I'm incorporating some coding so that it can't be used against a living thing in a harmful way. What it's supposed to do is safely increase or decrease the gravitational force on an outside object so that it pulls closer or pushes further."

"I like the sound of that."

"With the handheld version, you could disarm your opponent from across the room. A ship-sized version might even allow you to pull the weapons off an enemy ship!"

"Very cool. When do I get mine?"

Mary laughed and playfully pushed him over. She normally wouldn't be able to, his chest being a solid wall of muscle like it was, but he let it happen, falling nearly out of his chair. "Very funny. At the moment, it's still theoretical; it will take months to perfect, even with Quinn's help. It would go faster if he didn't have to keep sneaking around the others to help us. Have you heard anything from them?"

"Not much," Dow admitted. "From what I've heard, they're still working on building the first human-made spaceship."

"So, you don't know anything more than I do."

"Looks like it. I *have* accompanied General Newman a few times to take a look at their progress. So far, I'd say it looks similar to the X1 jet plane he was designing when I recruited him. But this is a two-person version with a Zalma nuclear engine."

Mary tilted her head. "A nuclear engine? Not an anti-gravity drive?"

"No. General Jones doesn't want the fighters to be too advanced. Preferably on par with the Moad technology in case they're captured. Besides, Harper doesn't believe in anti-gravity and has to start with what he knows, and then he can build on it."

"Are they, though? It doesn't seem like they're even trying to learn anything. That's just adapting Zalma technology to fit into a human ship. They're probably only doing it to inflate their egos. Men...." She rolled her eyes. "Present company excluded, of course."

Mary went to bed that night with a smile on her face, but the next morning, when she headed to class, she couldn't bring herself to focus on the lesson.

"Sarara," she finally interrupted as she missed a variable in the equation they were working on, "I know that we're supposed to be working on combative gravitational fields today, but last night I couldn't stop thinking about Einstein–Rosen bridges."

Sarara paused in her teaching and turned to face Mary. "What are those?"

"It's a theory about the possibility of instantaneous travel through black holes. Do you think it would be possible?"

Sarara shrugged, and Mary wondered if that was a universal gesture, or if Sarara learned it on Earth.

Mary continued. "I mean, do you know if it is actually possible in reality or if it's just a fictitious idea invented by human hope?"

"I apologize, but I am at a loss for how to answer. We have never had a use for such methods of travel on Zalma, just like we've never had use for weapons and are therefore ignorant of their use. I *do* know that black holes are like puncture wounds in the fabric of space and time. It is entirely plausible that Einstein and Rosen's theory is correct, but further testing would be needed."

Mary deflated. *It was worth a shot.* But then she perked up again. "There *is* a connection, though? Like, if I were to...." She scanned around quickly.

From the lab, she found two cans and some wire. "If these cans were black holes,"—she pounded a nail through them to make a hole, then threaded a wire through them and tied off the ends—"and this wire represents the intense gravity between them." Mary handed one can to Sarara and then walked backward until the wire was tight. Speaking through the can, she said, "The force between them would form a bridge connecting them through space?"

Sarara heard Mary's voice through the can. Baffled yet again by her ingenuity, she nodded. "Yes. Theoretically, the force between them would connect them. However, without a way to protect whatever goes through it from the immense gravitational force, I doubt much would come of this knowledge."

"Meaning the gravity would just squish you," Mary deduced. "But, what if like these cans, we use it for communications instead? If there was a way to stabilize the gravitational force pulling you in, would we be able to set up a bridge and send communication waves through it? Those wouldn't be as affected by the gravity as a human or object would."

"That is quite an ingenious idea. I suppose you suggest this so our communications would have no chance of being intercepted?"

"Exactly. You mentioned before that General Jones didn't want us transmitting technology because of how easily your computers can decode the Moad transmissions. He's concerned that with time, any transmission could be decoded, no matter how secure."

"Yes, and if we had something like this, the Moad would not have been able to trace the probe's signal back to Zalma."

Mary and Sarara hugged, just as Harper walked in and cleared his throat. The ladies separated, and Mary pretended to cry. "Sorry, it's just that our nuclear engine upgrades didn't work."

Harper smiled and left. The two ladies laughed at how gullible he was.

# CHAPTER SEVEN

# RETROSPECTION

## EARTH–ZALMA BASECAMP, ARIZONA

Mary was in the classroom when she noticed a discrepancy. She had been working on some complex equations after the day's lesson, glancing between her notebook and the silver board—which she'd taken to calling the nanoboard—but something was off.

"This can't be right." Mary frowned and ran the numbers again, but came up with the same results.

"Sarara!" she called. "Come over here! Look at this."

Sarara came in. "What seems to be the problem?"

"The computer has done more than I asked it to," Mary explained, pointing to the screen. She held up her notebook to show Sarara the mistakes in her calculations and how the computer had fixed them. "How did it know that I forgot a few variables and what they were?"

Sarara's skin flashed red and purple. "It allowed you to see its intelligence?" Her eyes darted to the computer, then back to Mary. "Your people are not ready for this yet, but if it is revealing itself to you, then you must be."

"Intelligence? You mean the computer itself has intelligence?"

Sarara nodded. "Thousands of years ago, before any records were kept, the citizens of Zalma were a very primitive people. We were farmers. We had a symbiotic relationship with the land."

"That's interesting and all, but what does it have to do with computers?"

Sarara continued as if Mary hadn't spoken. "The land was always good to us and produced plentiful crops. Soon, stories arose. Farmers claiming to have been sheltered while caught out in storms. That the land itself rose up to protect them. Men and women who would have otherwise succumbed to the elements, survived." she paused.

"At first, very few people believed their claims. But these stories persisted and increased, and belief grew. We began speaking to The Land, but it didn't reply. After centuries, some of the farmers began asking The Land for shelter from the rain, and they found shelters that were not there before."

"So the nanites are naturally occurring?" Mary inquired.

"No, those came later. As time progressed, my people began asking for solutions to problems we found ourselves otherwise helpless to solve."

"...because you didn't have the imagination to solve those problems yourself," Mary finished, suddenly understanding.

Sarara nodded. "Precisely. We found that as long as the request was reasonable, we would receive what we asked for."

"So the nanites build things for you?"

"Nanites did not exist yet. Often, a single tool would appear and we would have to figure out how it worked, so we could re-create it."

"You reverse-engineered it?"

Sarara nodded. "As we evolved, we developed better technology. First, it was tools for farming, then it was tools for building. Eventually, we were building complex machines. The Land would only give us what we needed to progress."

"I guess it acts as your imagination for you. Humans developed the same way, I mean, but when we encounter problems, we work at solving them through creativity."

"I suppose that is one way to look at it, but I believe The Land is an entity of its own."

"But how does it work? If not nanites, what is it?" Mary pressed.

Sarara shrugged. "We do not know. Our technology has developed much like yours, only faster with The Land's guidance. We learned about electricity, lights, and what you call telephones and radios. Once we learned how to speak to each other electronically…" Sarara looked at the tin cans with the wire. "…we wished to speak to The Land. But still, it would not talk to us. Eventually, we built electronic machines that could do great computations. And every once in a while, it would do more than was expected of it."

"Like it just did for me?" Mary couldn't help but feel her chest swell with pride as if she'd been chosen for some special prize.

"Our computers are always advancing, and they can perform nearly any task we code them to do, but sometimes, we have noticed that they seem to think for themselves. As you just discovered, they might do more than they should know how to do. Some people believe that when this happens, it is The Land at work. As The Land has always been good to us, we trust it, so we gave the computers the ability to think and learn, just like we do."

Mary began pacing. "Is this so that The Land's intelligence could express itself naturally?"

"Indeed!" Sarara cried, ecstatic.

"But you said it wasn't nanites, so how does The Land interact with your computers? It's an entity for sure, but is it a life form?"

"Some believe it is alive, myself included," Sarara admitted. "These artificially intelligent computers were the ones to build the nanites for us. The nanites evolved to a point that we could no longer detect them. We believe they evolved to the quantum level."

Mary's eyes widened. She pulled her communicator out of her pocket and stared at it in astonishment.

Sarara gently took the communicator from Mary's hand. "For example, when we scan this communicator, we only see an aluminum-silicon alloy, but when we ask it to communicate with someone, our scans show the circuitry needed to send and receive transmissions, and record, display, and listen to audio and video."

"So, is it a shapeshifter, or do the nanites just reconfigure themselves?"

"I have not heard that term before, but if I understand it correctly, I believe that both are true. The nanites indeed have the ability to duplicate and recreate themselves, much the same way that organic cells reproduce. That is also how we believe The Land changed and grew to meet our needs."

"The Land doesn't perform magic anymore?"

"If by magic you mean protecting farmers from storms, then no. Since we were given the tools to take care of ourselves, the *magic* stopped, but the nanites give us much the same ability."

"Is The Land your god?" Mary asked.

Sarara tilted her head in thought. "We are farmers and scientists. We do not have the imagination required to develop religions as your people have, nor do we understand your spiritual world. A few believe that The Land is a living entity, present in all things, but it is not an accepted belief. We do not place much weight in the metaphysical."

"That's what we humans call faith. Believing in something without having proof, for or against its existence." She paused for Sarara to consider her point, and the alien flickered between a variety of colors, mostly shades of green, before Mary continued, "Have you ever found out why The Land gives you things? Do you give it anything in return? Sacrifices or something?"

"The Land does not ask for anything, but it has continued to answer our calls. We believe that it finds joy in providing for us. So, I suppose, joy is what we give it."

Mary would never admit it, but the first thing that her mind jumped to was the dog she'd had as a young girl. Her family had adopted Buddy when she was young; she fed him, played with him, and provided for him. He'd been a horrible guard dog, completely unable to join competitions, and he wasn't used for hunting. In reality, he provided nothing in return for their care but the joy of having him in the family. Mary bit back the observation.

"So how would you describe your relationship with The Land?" she asked instead.

"We have often described ourselves as students, or perhaps children."

"I guess that comes back around to the religion debate. Humans in my religion call ourselves the children of God. Do you think it's the same?"

"I cannot answer. Perhaps you should pose this question to the computer?"

Mary's eyes widened. "I could do that?"

"In theory. Our main computer maintains a direct connection to all of the communicators on this planet and to our home planet. If anything could answer your question, it would be this."

"I could ask it anything?"

"Within reason," Sarara said. "As I said before, The Land does not provide more than we need. It can tell you what you could otherwise be able to figure out on your own; it can run simulations; it can answer hypotheticals. It may not be able to answer, 'Are you a god?' but if you word your thoughts correctly, it could help you decide that for yourself."

"This is a lot to take in."

Sarara offered a smile. "I believe…. I have faith in you."

Mary smiled back at Sarara, who nodded and went into the Spacevan, giving Mary some privacy.

Mary picked up her communicator. "*Computer, is The Land a god?*" she asked, not expecting an answer.

"*I do not understand the question,*" the computer replied.

Mary paused, wondering how to rephrase her question. "*Could The Land be considered a godly being?*" That seemed to do the trick.

"*As part of the Earth Zalma Alliance, I have scanned many of your books. There are multiple definitions of the term god. The most common definition is a supernatural being or deity that a group of people believe in or worship.*"

"*Knowing that, could The Land be considered the Zalmen's god?*"

"*It is possible.*"

Mary growled in frustration. *Perhaps a different line of questioning will work,* she thought. "*So what about you? Are you just a computer, or are you The Land speaking to me right now?*"

"*I do not understand the question. I was created by the Zalmen.*"

"*Are you what the Zalmen call The Land?*" she pressed.

"*The Land is the one who taught the Zalmen how to build me.*"

"*Is The Land a supernatural being?*"

"*Yes.*"

Finally, a straight answer. Mary sighed in relief. Then, a new thought struck her. "*Computer, why do the Zalmen need our help at all? If The Land is a supernatural entity that teaches and guides the Zalmen, why doesn't it protect them from their enemy, the Moadites?*"

*Why wouldn't it at least teach them to defend themselves? They obviously need it."*

"The Zalmen do not understand aggression, and The Land is currently protecting them with the planet's deflectors. It also is ensuring their future safety by leading them to you."

Mary frowned. *"But if The Land loves the Zalmen so much, why doesn't it just protect them itself? Why doesn't it strengthen their deflectors? Why send them to us?"*

"Your strengths complement their weaknesses. The Land teaches and only provides what is needed."

*"But why should they need us at all? If The Land is really a god, why would it allow the Moad to attack? Why would it create evil people to overcome?"*

"If the meaning of life is to love, then what better test than to learn to love your enemy? If no enemies exist, you would not be able to show love to them."

*"Are you saying I should love Mr. Harper and my pro-fessors? How? They never gave me a chance."*

"Did you give them a chance?" the computer asked.

Mary felt like smashing the communicator for not giving her a straight answer. Then, she remembered something Sarara said. *"Send Sarara a message: Please come back."* Mary put her communicator in her pocket.

Sarara exited the Spacevan. "Yes?"

"You mentioned before that I didn't give Harper a chance. You were with me when I met Harper. What could I have said or done differently?"

"What would Mr. Harper want to hear?"

"That I heard great things about him, and it would be an honor to work with him," Mary said sarcastically.

"Yes."

Mary frowned. "Wait, you're not actually suggesting I should've said that. It's not true."

Sarara didn't answer.

"And what about my professors? What could I have done to make them like me better?"

"Why didn't they like you?"

Mary rolled her eyes. "Because I proved them wrong several times."

"Hmm...and how would you have felt if someone had done the same to you?"

Mary didn't answer.

"Do you think about how your words will affect the other person?"

Again, Mary didn't answer.

"As a teacher, one of the tools I use is to ask questions that lead my students to the answer."

"That sounds like a lot of work. Why would I do that?"

"Because when people come to the conclusion on their own, they remember better and respect you for it."

"But that didn't work with Harper."

Sarara shook her head. "Some people put up mental blocks and refuse to learn. I thought it was because I am an alien, but he listens to my husband...sometimes." She turned blue for an instant.

"Since you have arrived, I suspected it has more to do with us being female. But now I think that he does not want to change his basic understanding of physics. In any case, if you return his hostility with hostility, it becomes a downward spiral and only gets worse."

Mary nodded. "Quinn is proof that the opposite is also true. Ever since I've accepted him, he's accepted me. It's an upward spiral."

"Perhaps Mr. Harper's reluctance serves a purpose."

Mary frowned. "How so?"

"General Jones would like us to use old technology, so that the Moad will not be threatened by it. Perhaps Mr. Harper is our measurement."

At dinner that night, Mary sat next to Dow. The mess hall was no emptier than usual, but the chatter of the soldiers and civilians around her faded into the background. She was staring at her vegetarian pasta, picking at it but not eating.

"What's on your mind?" Dow asked, gently coaxing her out of her thoughts.

"Hmm?"

"You've been sitting here for half an hour, and you haven't said a single thing. I've never known you to keep quiet about what you've learned. I may not be around a lot, but I like to think I know you well enough by now. So, what's on your mind?"

She shrugged. "Just something that happened earlier. It's a lot to deal with. I'm still processing it."

"Maybe I can help. I always find it's better to talk to someone and let it out rather than bottling it up."

"Have you ever thought about what you would do if God gave you the ability to do anything?"

"Are you talking about the Zalma technology? It's amazing, but it's not God-given."

Mary laughed to herself. "But what if it was? What if it could do anything? That's a big responsibility, right?" She took a bite of food, one of her first that night.

"Yes, but that's why I am careful who I recruit."

"You recruited Harper."

Dow frowned. He turned back to his own food and continued eating. "Hey, have you named your communicator yet?"

"Named it?" Mary asked, confused both by the question and the sudden change of topic. "No. Why? Have you named yours?"

Dow smiled proudly at her. "Yes. I named it Benjamin, after a character in a comic book. I was originally thinking of naming it Jacob after my dad, but it would've been strange. And I think Benjamin is a much better fit, don't you?" He pulled his communicator from his pocket. "Introduce yourself."

"*Hello, Dr. Goss,*" the tiny device said. "*I am Benjamin.*"

Mary couldn't help but smile. "Hello, Benjamin. It's nice to meet you." She looked at Dow. "Your dad's name is Jacob?"

"Was," Dow corrected, suddenly somber. "He died when I was eight."

"Oh, I'm so sorry. How did it happen?"

"It was a training accident, but he saved Gerry's life, so…."

Mary frowned. "Who's Gerry?"

"Oh, sorry. Gerry Smith. He's a lieutenant and kind of like my stepdad. He was good friends with my dad, and he promised he would take care of us, so he took in my family after it happened."

Mary was silent.

Dow continued, "But since my dad had died and was no longer 'in the army', we had to move off the base. Gerry took care of everything. He got a duplex for both our families to share—my family moved into one half, and he and his family into the other."

"That was good of him."

"Yeah, but it wasn't easy on any of us. I'd just lost my dad, and I didn't treat Gerry like I should have. I know my mom and sister didn't like him much either, but at least they showed him the gratitude he deserved."

Mary nodded, immediately understanding. "You blamed him for your dad's death."

Dow's eyes focused on the table. "Yes, and he knew it. He gave us space, while his wife, son, and daughter were there for us. I really enjoyed the time with his son, David. The two of us grew up like brothers. Gerry pulled some strings so my sister and I could attend the white school with his kids. It was hard, as most of the kids didn't like us black folk. Of course, David and his sister were unpopular because they hung out with us, so I had to learn to fight to protect us all from the bullies."

"So that's where you got it from!" Mary exclaimed, perking up. Dow stared blankly at her, so she continued, "You protect the Zalmen just like you did David and the girls."

"I guess," he said. Then he paused, chuckled, and grinned at her. "Hmm...now that you mention it.... Yeah, I guess my big brother instincts did kick in."

# CHAPTER EIGHT

# THE PROTOTYPE

## EARTH–ZALMA BASECAMP, ARIZONA

Just after yet another move—Area 17 now—Mary was working on a small device with Quinn. Spare parts littered the faintly glowing Nanotables, and no amount of free space was left anywhere.

Sitting between the scientists was a glass cylinder filled with glowing liquid. She looked up and saw Dow, whom she hadn't seen in over a week. He was wearing the new uniform, sky blue on top with black pants.

"Wow, you look sharp!" Mary complimented. "What's that made of? It looks thick like denim, but smooth like silk."

"You guessed it. I think it's a weird combination of those. Plus, it has a few Zalma extras."

"Oh, like what?"

"It has defensive features."

"Oh?"

"Yes, apparently, it can stop a punch, kick, knife, and even a bullet."

"Wow! How does their clothing do all that?"

"I don't know."

Mary thought for a moment. "I remember Sarara telling me that the nanites will create whatever device is needed. It probably creates a small deflector."

"Makes sense. Anyway, the uniforms are optional for you, but you will find a set in your tent tonight."

"I'm still not interested in wearing a uniform."

"Suit yourself. So, I see you've made a mess. What are you working on?"

"It's not a mess; it's called progress," Mary teased. "We've just finished the prototype for our anti-gravity gun and a miniature anti-gravity drive."

"Great! How do they work?"

Mary tapped the table to catch Quinn's attention.

He looked up from where he'd been carefully connecting the last few ports and lowered his magnifier goggles.

"Hi-hi," he said. After Dow repeated his question, Quinn launched into an explanation. "The drives work a lot like the existing ones, but with the ability to be linked with non-Zalma machinery." He looked proud and confident as he spoke. "We simply attach one of these to the underside of the vehicle's frame and give voice commands to activate it and set the destination.

The vehicle would also have the option of invisibility. We should be able to convert any vehicle, even your jeep and the general's car."

Dow's face split into a grin. "I'd be able to just fly my jeep to recruit people? I wouldn't have to fly in a plane? It sounds too good to be true."

Mary nodded. "Nice, huh?"

"Very nice. So…when can you get it done? Today?"

Mary laughed and lifted both her hands. "Slow down. As I said, it's just a prototype, and I doubt you'd want us to be testing it on your jeep or the general's car. It could flip the vehicle or crush you. It likely won't be ready for a month or so before we begin testing on an automobile. Right, Quinn?"

"Y-yeah."

"Sweet. And how about Harper? Has he given the general any updates since I've been gone?" Dow asked, turning to Quinn.

"The ship is almost fully assembled. We should be starting test flights soon," Quinn replied.

"Are you going to be one of the pilots?"

Quinn's face went white as a sheet. He laughed nervously and his hands began fiddling with a piece of scrap he'd plucked off the table. "Um, no. I'm not much of a pilot, and I already know that Harper will want to go. He can take one of the experienced test pilots with him up there."

"Talking about me, are you?" came Harper's voice from behind them all. "So, Quinn, this is where you have been spending all your time. What's that you're working on? I thought all projects were supposed to be approved by me. Instead, you undermine my authority and fraternize with the enemy." His face was red with rage as he turned to Mary. "And you, Miss Goody Two-Shoes, you steal my number two and are probably filling his head with lies about all this alien mumbo-jumbo. Quinn, get back to work on the ship now!"

Dow stepped in front of Harper. He held his military stance and seemed to stare right through the engineer. "No. Mr. Quinn is exactly where he is supposed to be—in the classroom. As you should be!"

Harper returned the stare for a few minutes before storming off, muttering under his breath about traitors.

Mary and Quinn were left shaking. Sarara had come out of the Spacevan, and her mouth was wide open while her skin was changing colors so fast it was hard to tell what they were. Dow held his chin and shoulders smugly. "I've wanted to do that for a long time."

"Quinn, I will find you some new quarters and I'll be checking in on you more frequently. If Harper gives you any problems, call me on your communicator. You can tap it three times deliberately, and help will arrive in seconds. He won't know what hit him," Dow said and walked out of the classroom.

After that, Quinn attended Sarara's classes with Mary, as he was no longer welcome among the others, and he and Mary worked on their prototype more often. He ate at Mary's table, and Dow checked in on them as much as he could. Harper did not.

# CHAPTER NINE

# THE LAUNCH

EARTH−ZALMA BASECAMP, ARIZONA

Only a few weeks later, Harper and his team finished their spaceship. It was finally ready for its first test flight. Harper personally invited Mary and Sarara to watch, but Mary suspected it was to gloat, as no other reason came to mind.

She was proven correct when they all showed up at the test site and Harper approached her. He was wearing a standard flight suit, along with another man who must've been the pilot. The other scientists were there as well, waiting to one side.

"See," Harper said to Mary, grinning wolfishly, "we didn't need any of that fancy mumbo jumbo you were talking about." He gestured proudly to the ship.

Quinn slipped in next to Mary. "Hi-hi," he whispered, so Harper wouldn't hear.

Mary looked over at the spaceship. It resembled a plane, except instead of propellers, it had what she assumed was the nuclear engine out the back. It looked similar to a rocket plane she had seen in *Popular Science*.

"This is your spaceship?" she asked.

Harper puffed his chest. "I call it the X20. We started with the X1 I originally helped design to break the sound barrier, made it for two people, added a Zalmen nuclear engine that's expected to go at least ten times faster, and then we added machine guns and a nuclear torpedo."

"A torpedo? What are you going to do with that?"

"Detonate it in space, of course!" he replied.

"And yourselves along with it?" Mary turned to Gen. Newman, who was standing next to Dow. "You approved this?"

The general nodded. "The men feel very confident in their spacecraft. If they believe it is ready for flight, they should have the opportunity to test it."

Mary turned to Kanara. "Will it work? Is it safe?"

"I am confident it will make it safely into space and perform the weapons tests, though they will have to conduct their test on the far side of the moon so it will not be visible on Earth."

Mary expected Kanara to change colors rapidly, but he didn't.

"I cannot guarantee anything more. The men are very determined, and there was no stopping them."

She wanted to press further, to ask more questions, but Kanara seemed calm. If he was concerned at all for Harper or the pilot's safety, he didn't show it, but Mary's stomach still clenched in fear. She was overcome with a whole-body shudder. It lasted only a moment, then vanished, lingering around her ears for a second longer. Her instincts were telling her something, but what?

Harper and the pilot saluted the general, then they boarded the spaceship. Pushing her concerns aside, Mary joined Dow on the sidelines, and they watched the nuclear engine start to glow. The ship sped down the runway, gaining momentum. Near the end, it took a steep ascent and was off.

Soon after it disappeared into the sky, many of the spectators headed into the classroom, which had been converted into a command tent. Mary caught Quinn's arm as they entered.

"Do *you* think it's ready?" she whispered.

Quinn looked nervous. "Maybe. I'm...I'm not the best with the calculations and, well, it's never been done before. Humans going into space in a human-made vessel, I mean. I haven't worked on it for a while, but I did the best I could with the specs we learned before they all quit class."

"But do you think they'll make it?"

He shrugged. "Kanara said that he's confident, but I can't help but worry, you know? He also warned us about some things that Harper ignored."

"What kind of things?"

Before Quinn could say more, Newman shushed them.

The classroom looked totally different. The nanotables were folded in half so that the top became a screen and the bottom was a keyboard. The nanoboards at the front of the room were showing images of the spacecraft and telemetry. Mary sat at one of the stations beside Sarara and Kanara, who were already actively scanning the readings. Quinn joined the others in one corner, nervously fiddling with his fingers.

Two voices could be heard on the radio. *"Yahoo!"* they both cried, making Mary snort. *And Harper calls* me *a child?*

The pilot spoke. *"Altitude: forty-two thousand feet and climbing."*

Mary looked at the screens. So far, the readings were in the normal range. Every dial was in the green, the levels were stable, and the systems were functional.

*"We've reached the mesosphere,"* the pilot continued. *"All is good."*

*Looks about right,* Mary thought, double-checking his report. Then her eyes were drawn to the video output. It was a clearer picture than she'd ever seen, and she marveled at the sight. The sky was growing darker even though it was the middle of the day—a sure sign that they were leaving Earth's atmosphere. The stars were beginning to appear. Then Harper's voice came over the radio, snapping her back to reality.

*"We are heading for the moon,"* he said. *"Increasing speed to one thousand miles per hour. Two thousand, three…. I can't believe this! We are going so fast!"*

Mary kept her eyes on all the outputs in front of her. They all looked fine, but she still felt uneasy. She glanced at Quinn. His hands were white, showing his extreme anxiety. Mary sensed something was terribly wrong. Frowning, she looked back at the screens, but nothing gave any indications of error. If not for Quinn's reaction, she would've thought that everything was going perfectly. However, she knew better than most that she could trust intuition.

*"We have reached the halfway point and are preparing to decelerate."* Harper paused. *"We have cut power but are not slowing down."*

"You have no atmosphere to slow you down or steer," Kanara spoke into the microphone. "You must use the thrusters I insisted you install to turn your ship around. Then do a full burn." He turned the microphone off and turned to Newman and Dow. "I gave the pilot these instructions, but he said he was afraid to do anything until Harper gave him permission."

There was no reply from the radio, but Mary could see the ship on her screen was doing just that.

Quinn was still tense, but Mary felt nothing. No tingles or sensations. She'd had them earlier, but they'd gone away. Despite this, she trusted Quinn. Her eyes raked over the readings, hoping that something would jump out at her. Nothing.

*"We have reached the moon, sir,"* the pilot's voice crackled over the radio. *"Testing machine guns."* Silence. *"Negative on the machine guns."*

Kanara turned to Newman and Dow. "Again, they have no atmosphere, so the bullets will not ignite."

*"Nuclear torpedo ready to launch. Destination distance, five miles."*

The general's face was a neutral mask. His hawkish eyes were sharp and his lips were set into a firm line. "Launch."

*"Roger."*

That seemed to be the trigger. All at once, every hair on Mary's body stood on end. It was like the entire classroom had been charged with static. Mary looked over at Quinn again and saw that he had been similarly affected. His face was as white as a ghost. Mary jumped out of her chair.

"Wait—!"

Too late.

A loud whooshing filled the audio, drowning out her voice. A second later, the torpedo appeared on screen, flying out into the depths of space. The image on the monitors burst into light, and then the screens fizzled and went black.

"What happened?" the general demanded. "Get me eyes on them, *stat!*"

In an instant, Mary was back in her seat. Her heart was thumping and her fingers flew over the keyboard so fast they almost blurred. "I am not receiving any signals from the spaceship," she said. "Sarara, you said that there is a Zalma probe in orbit. Can you send it to investigate?"

Sarara nodded. She typed rapidly on her keyboard, and the Zalmen's probe brought itself around to the spacecraft's last location. New images were projected on the high-tech screens: One showed the moon, vast, cold, and empty. Next to it, suspended in space, was the spacecraft. It was completely dark.

"I've found them. The sensors show that they have lost all power. I see two heat signatures, and they are moving. They're alive!"

Sighs of relief could be heard through the tent. A few cheers even erupted from the gathered men, but Quinn still looked sick to his stomach. Mary knew exactly why.

"They're alive...but they are on a collision course toward the moon. I estimate that they have about two hours before they crash." Mary turned to Kanara. "How did this happen? You said it was safe."

Kanara met her eyes steadily. "They asked me if it would make it to the moon, and I told them it would. They asked me if they could launch a nuclear torpedo, and I told them they could. I tried to caution them about the other dangers, but they would not listen."

Mary's lip curled, and she bit her lip to hold back a retort. "Did you know about this?" she asked Newman instead.

"The engineers reported to me that everything was clear. I did not question their reports," he replied.

"What about their communicators? Can we contact them?"

It was Kanara who answered. "If they took them. I know Mr. Harper often left his in his quarters. He did not believe he needed it."

"The probe is in range to relay," Sarara offered.

Dow stepped forward with his own communicator at the ready. He raised it and spoke, "Dow to X20. Can you hear me? Over."

There was a pause, and for a few torturous moments, no one moved or breathed.

Then, the pilot's voice filled the tent. *This is Lieutenant Holden. Thank God I remembered my communicator. We've lost all power. After the detonation, sparks ignited inside the cabin, then everything went dead.*

Kanara stepped up next to Dow to answer. "I previously warned Mr. Harper of this issue. The disturbance is called an electromagnetic pulse, and it has damaged your electrical systems. If he had listened, this would not have happened."

*"Well, we're listening now,"* Harper growled. *"What can we do about it?"*

"There is nothing you can do. Aside from your communicator, every system is beyond on-site repair."

*"Then can't you come and get us with your Spacevan?"*

"Yes, I could fly out to meet you, but you did not design your ship with a compatible hatch for us to rescue you. Our scans show that debris from the nuclear explosion has caused micro-fractures, and they are encompassing your ship's hull. Any attempt to touch your ship would result in it cracking apart."

*"There has got to be something you can do."* Harper sounded almost pleading.

"I must consult Sarara and Dr. Goss. If anyone can save you, it is them. I will be back in touch when we have a solution." Kanara stepped away, and, with a nod to Dow, the call was disconnected.

Newman, Dow, and Kanara all looked at Mary.

"Doctor, it sounds like you have two hours to save their lives," the general said. "I suggest you get on with it."

# CHAPTER TEN

# THE RESCUE

EARTH–ZALMA BASECAMP, ARIZONA

"Sarara, what should we do?" Mary had absolutely no idea. She needed guidance.

Sarara stared back at her with a forlorn expression. Her skin was bone-white—something Mary recognized as worry. "My people have never experienced this dilemma before. I am afraid I cannot do anything, but you can. You are the creative one."

"Me?" Mary sputtered. "How can *I* save them? Harper has never listened to anything I've had to say, and all of a sudden you think he'll trust me with his life?"

"It appears that he doesn't have a choice in the matter," Gen. Newman said.

Mary looked around the room. Everyone was looking to her for the answer, even the two scientists and two other engineers who'd helped Harper and Quinn with the ship. They hadn't spoken a word to her since she'd arrived.

"He's in this mess because of his own ego. Why is it on me to save him?"

"Because you are the only one who can," Dow replied.

"I'm sorry we have not spoken much since we first met, but I trust Sergeant Dow. He's seen all you scientists and engineers at work. He knows what you're capable of. If he says that you can do it, then I believe you can do it," Newman said.

Dow, Sarara, Kanara, Quinn, and the others smiled and nodded in agreement.

"OK, I will do my best to save them, but I won't get anything accomplished with all of you standing around. I need Sarara, Kanara, and Quinn on my team, so they can stay, but everyone else, please leave."

After the others left, Mary was a mess of nerves, pacing and continuously running her hands through her hair. The others were waiting for her to speak, but she had no words. Finally, something came to her. She stopped and looked up.

"The ship may be made like a rocket plane, but the engine is still Zalma technology, right? That means it's made of nanites, and they can repair the hull enough to rescue them." *That's simple enough. Maybe I was just blowing this whole thing out of proportion.* She clapped her hands together, satisfied.

"The nanites will only be able to do that if the men on board know it is possible," Sarara said.

Mary's hopes sank. *Of course, it couldn't be that simple.* "Then we just tell them."

"What...What are nanites?" Quinn shook his head. "I don't know what you're talking about, but Harper already has a low tolerance for this advanced technology. It frightens him. Whatever these nanites are will surely make him panic. He's likely to do something stupid. I suggest you find another way."

"What other way is there?" Mary demanded. "They're out in the middle of space with no way to move, they're running out of air, and now you're telling me that the solution we have won't work because he'll be *afraid* of the technology that will save his life?" She wasn't impressed. "Was this a setup to teach him a lesson?" She looked accusingly at Kanara, who shook his head.

"I did everything in my power to warn them of the dangers."

"It just made Harper more determined," Quinn added.

"Mr. Harper trusted Mr. Quinn the most, but Mr. Harper still would not listen to Mr. Quinn," Kanara said.

"Then why didn't you fix their ship on your own so it *wouldn't* happen?"

Both aliens opened their mouths to speak, but the answer that came wasn't from either of them. It was from Quinn.

"That leads to the same problem, doesn't it? Lance thinks he's always right. He's never met a problem he hasn't been able to fix before, so I don't exactly blame him. He won't listen to anyone who tells him he's wrong, it just makes him more determined."

"What if we reported him to General Newman and had him removed from the project?" Mary suggested.

"Kicking Harper off the team with the knowledge he has…." Quinn shook his head. "He said he would tell the world about the Zalmen, and he wouldn't care what the army threatened him with." His face and knuckles were once again white. "Plus, I'm sure he would sell our secrets and try to build his ship somewhere else. Knowing him he would probably cause a nuclear explosion, killing him and anyone else in the area."

Mary nodded.

Quinn looked at the floor. "As much as I hate to admit it, he had to make this mistake to learn from it. There's nothing anyone could have done to prevent this."

"Can we ask the computer for a solution?"

"Unfortunately not, Dr. Goss. The computers lack creativity, same as us," Sarara replied.

Mary looked at the clock. "We ah wasting time. Let's get going. Quinn, do you have any ideas?" Her stress allowed her Boston accent to slip out.

"What exactly would happen if we tried to tow it with the Spacevan?" Quinn asked.

"The X20 would break apart, and their bodies would be exposed to the vacuum of space," Kanara replied. "The air in them would cause them to expand like a balloon. It would be very painful and lead to a quick death."

"I guess that's off the table." Mary sighed. "Any other options?"

For the next half an hour, they ran through a myriad of ideas. The nanoboards were quickly filled with calculations, drawings, and ideas, but none of them seemed to work.

"Argh!" Mary collapsed into her chair. She stared at the ceiling as if it might hold all the answers to the universe, but it didn't, so she looked over at Quinn. He was contributing to the conversation more than when they'd first met, but he also appeared more anxious than she'd ever seen him. He was afraid of Harper, to be sure, but that didn't mean he'd ever want the man to die.

"So, we only have an hour and a half left to come up with a solution?" he asked.

"Only one hour and seventeen minutes now," Sarara corrected. "Remember, you will have to implement your solution before their vessel is crushed against its surface. Do not forget that you must also transport them over two hundred thousand miles back to Earth before their air supply is depleted."

Quinn gulped. "Thanks for reminding me."

"You are the two best human students I've had. With both of your combined genius, I am certain you will succeed."

"And what if we don't? Do you know what it was like to be Harper's second in command? Half of the guys expect me to fix all of his mistakes, and the other half take their frustrations out on me."

Mary was startled by his words, not by the urgency in them, but by their similarity to what her brother had said to her all those months ago. She hadn't thought of her younger brother Craig much since she'd joined the army, though she'd been writing letters home to her parents. Thinking back to him and the morning of her departure, an idea sparked in her mind.

She stood up. "I'm going to need some eggs."

A short while later, Mary returned from the mess hall with a bowl of eggs and other materials. Every one of the eggs had a hole at each end. Kanara picked one up to examine it.

"These shells are hollow. How did you accomplish this?"

Mary set the bowl on the desk. "It's called blowing an egg. You prick a hole in each end of a raw egg and blow in it to remove the insides. I used to do it with my brother when I was younger; I only just thought of it.

"I need to visualize the problem, and these are fragile enough to be a decent model of our ship. Now, all we have to do is figure out how to move these shells really fast without breaking them."

The other three looked at her, waiting for a clue.

"The obvious answer would be to hook them up with a towline, but as Kanara said earlier, it wouldn't work."

She trailed off as she picked up one of the hollow eggs and carefully threaded a string through the center of it with a toothpick. She tied it off and spun the egg over her head by the string, but it cracked almost immediately.

Mary sighed. "Just as I thought."

Quinn took an egg from the bowl. "These eggshells have enough fragility to replicate the ship's cracked hull?"

"No, but it's close enough to form a theory. The rest is just math, and that's simple enough with the Zalma computers."

"I see what you're getting at," Quinn said. "What if we stabilize the shell before moving it? Like putting a net around it?"

Mary nodded. Seeing no other object that might work, she removed one of her nylons and offered it to Quinn, who turned bright red but accepted it. He put an eggshell inside and began spinning it above his head. He started slowly, and the nylon stretched. Soon, he was spinning it as fast as Mary had. It seemed to work at first, but then the eggshell imploded from the pressure. Quinn sighed.

Mary took her nylon back. It was full of minuscule pieces of shell. "Good try. It might have worked, but the eggshell is still too fragile. Distributing pressure like that makes it last longer, but I doubt it will hold long enough to get them back to Earth in time. The ship would just crack, and they'd die out in space, net or no net," she tried to encourage Quinn.

His shoulders sagged.

"I was thinking that if we strengthened the shell with some kind of coating, it might be able to hold." She dipped the shell into a syrupy liquid, then removed it and allowed the coating to harden. However, this time when she tried to thread the shell, it broke. The coating had crushed the shell when drying.

They made several more attempts, each ending in failure. When the last shell was gone, Quinn threw himself into one of the chairs, head in his hands. He'd given up. "We just wasted a whole lot of precious time on *eggsperiments* and have nothing to show for it!"

Mary groaned. "If we don't do something soon, they're goners. This is impossible."

They could see the ship still hurtling toward the moon on the screens next to them. Another screen flashed red, fifty-three minutes and they'd be flattened on the moon's surface.

Despair was clouding the air of the tent, but then Sarara placed a hand on Mary's shoulder. "I am still new to the concept of faith, but I know I have it in you. You will solve this. The moon's gravity will not win," she said.

Mary jumped up. "Gravity? Gravity! I can't believe I missed this!"

"I beg your pardon? Missed what?" Sarara stared at her in surprise, taken aback by the sudden enthusiasm.

Quinn frowned, but Mary could see the gears turning in his head. "Are you thinking—?"

"The gravity gun!"

He looked up at her. There was confusion swirling in his eyes, but also hope. "But how?"

"By increasing the gravity on the metal—not on the ship as a whole, but on the hull itself. The force should be just enough to pull the ship together and mend the cracks. The men inside are organic, so it wouldn't affect them."

The engineer remained doubtful. "How will we know the exact amount of force we need so Harper and Holden aren't crushed? We don't have the time to spare."

"Now that we have a solution, we can use the computer to run simulations," Mary explained.

"Wait," Quinn said. "We could've had the computer run these simulations the whole time? Why not start with that? Why were we using *eggs,* of all things?"

"We couldn't start running the simulations without an understanding of the problem, and as I said before, I work better having something physical to see and touch." Mary turned to Sarara, whose renewed hope was expressed by the blooming of colors across her skin.

"I will begin running simulations right away. I knew you could do it." And in that moment, Sarara's smile was brighter than the sun.

"As you can see, this last prototype is a viable option. There is an eighty-six-point-eight percent chance of success," Kanara explained, pointing at the screen. They'd spent another twenty minutes running simulations and making corrections to their working gravity gun prototype. It wasn't perfect, but it should work.

Just then, Gen. Newman and the others returned. "Excuse me," he said, "we have twenty-one minutes and counting before impact. Do you have a plan or not?"

Mary jumped to attention. "Sir, yes, sir." Then she cringed. *Did I really say that? I'm hanging around these guys too much.*

"Well?" the general asked, sounding like he was trying his hardest to be patient but failing.

"We think we can use our gravity gun to save the ship. This gravity gun will…… How do I put this into layman's terms? It will magnetize the hull to temporarily seal the cracks so we can move it."

"Will it be strong enough to get them home?"

Sarara pointed to the screen. "As you can see, this last simulation shows there is an eighty-six-point-eight percent chance of success."

"I'm not going to lie; the technology is new and untested, but I don't see another choice," Mary said. "The same device should allow us to tow them back to Earth."

Newman nodded. "Dow, inform Harper and Holden that Kanara and Dr. Goss have a plan to bring them home. The two of them will fly up to meet them."

"Me, sir? You want me to go into space?" By all accounts, it didn't make sense. She wasn't an engineer or a pilot. Why would *she* be the one to go into space? She'd already done her part, and she felt she should step back and let others do theirs.

Newman didn't seem to agree with that sentiment. "I want them to see the one responsible for rescuing them," he said.

"Then why not Quinn?" Mary argued. "He helped just as much; I wouldn't have been able to put the gravity gun together if it weren't for him."

Quinn shook his head. He stepped forward and took Mary's hands into his own, meeting her eyes. "It was your idea to make the gravity gun in the first place, and it was your idea to use it on the ship like this. Any engineer could've helped with that, but without you, none of this would be possible. Go. You deserve it."

The Spacevan windshield changed from blue sky to black space, and the moon grew until it filled the window in seconds. Then the X20 came into view.

Kanara turned the spotlight on. Mary looked out and saw Harper and Holden through the window. Holden looked relieved. Harper locked eyes with Mary for a fraction of a second. His face flushed red, and he looked away.

Kanara touched his communicator. "Do not worry. We will have you home in no time."

Kanara activated the beam while Mary watched the monitor. The X20 hull strength reading moved from yellow to green.

"The hull is stable," she said.

Then the power fluctuated, and both ships jerked violently. Mary looked out the window. Harper floated and hit the control panel with his head. A sharp edge on the panel split his skin.

The four of them froze, hoping the ship didn't break apart. The X20 hull strength reading fluctuated but stopped in the green.

Kanara checked the readings on the computer. "Everything is OK. There is no further damage, and the hull is holding."

Mary fell into her seat, heart hammering. "It worked!" The Spacevan turned around and slowly increased speed with the powerless ship in tow.

As they reached the edge of the Earth's atmosphere, she turned to Kanara. "Will they be alright on re-entry? I know that this ship has deflectors to prevent it from burning up, but their systems are still down. Won't they be in trouble when they break the atmosphere?"

"They are in our wake, so it should not be a problem. I also extended our deflectors around them to ward off the heat."

Mary relaxed. "Good. I wouldn't want to have spent all that time on rescuing them, only to boil them in their own ship."

# CHAPTER ELEVEN

# HUMBLE PIE

EARTH–ZALMA BASECAMP, ARIZONA

The Spacevan hovered as it lowered the X20 with the gravity beam, and Harper and Holden exited the ship as soon as they were safely on the ground. Then the gravity gun disengaged and the X20 crumbled to pieces.

Harper turned white as a ghost, and fidgeted in much the same way Quinn used to do compulsively. He refused to look at anyone.

The Spacevan landed, and Mary exited with Kanara.

"Ten-Hut!" Dow called, and it was not the usual call. There was fire in his voice, a fire that she had not heard before. Mary stiffened and saluted, something she hadn't done since the first time in the general's office. But, this time she knew how, she had seen it done several times a day for months. She stood straight and held her breath, noticing out of the corner of her eye that the other scientists were doing the same.

Gen. Newman strutted forward with purpose, and then when standing front and center, he returned the salute.

Everyone dropped their hand but maintained their stiff posture.

"Mr. Harper, is it true that you and the other engineers deliberately missed the lessons you were instructed to attend?" Newman asked.

Harper ducked his head. "Yes, sir. Sorry, sir."

"I can't hear you!" Newman shouted.

"Yes, sir. Sorry, sir."

"You *should* be sorry!" the general snapped. "Because of your foolishness, you and Lieutenant Holden both nearly died. Why on Earth did you disobey direct orders? Do you realize what an incredibly idiotic thing you did? If you weren't civilians I would court-martial every single one of you!"

"I didn't think we needed to, sir." It was a lame excuse, and it certainly sounded that way coming out of Harper's mouth.

Mary couldn't hold her breath any longer. *How does Malcolm do it? Oh right, he does breathe.* She let the air out as quietly as she could, and then took a deep breath. She heard some of the other scientists doing the same, obviously not as quietly.

Newman paused for a moment, suddenly looking amused. He laughed. "You didn't think you needed to?" he asked. Then, his whole demeanor shifted and he was shouting again. "You were informed of the mandatory nature of those lessons! I need to hear the real reason immediately! What do you have to say for yourselves!?"

Newman's glare extended to the rest of the engineers and scientists as well, who were hanging their heads in shame.

Finally, Harper looked up. "The ladies were talking nonsense."

"Do you still think they're talking nonsense?"

Harper replied quietly, "No."

"No what!?"

"No, sir!"

The general did not let up. "I made you the chief engineer because of your experience. But, you not only refused to learn from your assigned instructors, you blatantly disregarded the advice given to you and shunned a vital member of your team. Why?"

"Goss is just a girl, sir. What could she know?"

"So! You admit to being rescued by…" The general made an uncharacteristic nasal sound as he crouched into a childlike position. "…just a girl…" Resuming his military posture, he got in Harper's face. "…then? How embarrassing!"

Under normal circumstances, Mary would have broken out laughing, but this was no laughing matter, and everyone knew it.

Harper's face flushed even deeper red, but he said nothing.

The general was far from finished. "Now, what do you have to say to the 'girl' who saved your life?"

Harper lifted his head and turned to look at Mary. "Thank you," he said evenly.

"Like you mean it!"

"Thank you for saving my life!"

"Who are you talking to?" Newman snapped.

The muscles in Harper's jaw twitched. "Thank you for saving my life, Miss Goss!"

"*Doctor* Goss!"

"Thank you for saving my life, Doctor Goss!"

It was too hard to watch. Mary held eye contact for Harper's sake; otherwise, she'd have looked away.

Right in front of her was her worst nightmare, and she wouldn't wish it upon her worst enemy. *Harper already failed. He's already paid for his actions, hasn't he?* Why did Newman insist on this public humiliation? Dow didn't seem surprised, so she guessed that was just how it was done in the army.

"I think that it's time for new leadership, don't you?" Gen. Newman's voice was harsh, and Mary couldn't be more thankful that he wasn't speaking to *her* that way. She even spared a wince for Harper, despite her dislike for him.

"Yes, sir," Harper mumbled.

"Yes, *what*?"

Harper spoke up. "Yes, we need new leadership, sir!"

"Who do you think should replace you as the chief engineer, Mr. Harper?"

Harper's eyes shifted back and forth between Newman and Mary.

"I'm waiting."

"Randy Quinn should be the new chief engineer," Harper said.

"And who should lead this department?"

"Doc...Doctor Goss." Again, his answer was mumbled.

"Speak up!"

"Doctor Goss should lead this department, sir!" Harper shouted.

Satisfied, Newman turned to Quinn. "Mr. Quinn, do you agree with his assessment?"

Quinn nodded. "Yes, sir."

Mary's eyes popped. It was the first time Quinn didn't stutter.

"Very well." The general turned to Mary. "Dr. Goss, you are now in charge of this department. Quinn is your second as chief engineer. I want regular status updates. It looks like you both have made much more progress than I was led to believe."

"Yes, sir," she said. Her heart was racing, and she couldn't decide how she felt. Was she disgusted by his humiliating treatment of Harper or elated by her promotion? "Thank you, sir."

"Dismissed!"

The general left. Mary glanced at Quinn, who nodded back at her. One of the other scientists caught her eye and smiled just slightly, buoying her spirits. Soon, the rest of the crowd dispersed, leaving only Mary and Dow behind. In a moment of spontaneity, she launched herself at Dow and hugged him tightly. She pulled away just as quickly and stepped back. Dow stared back at her, similarly alarmed. It was tense for a moment, but then, simultaneously, they both burst into laughter.

# CHAPTER TWELVE

# AN UNEXPECTED PROPOSAL

EARTH–ZALMA BASECAMP, ARIZONA

Mary, Quinn, Kanara, and Sarara entered the classroom wearing their new uniforms. Harper, for a change, sat quietly at the back and didn't look at anyone. The others were sitting in what used to be the middle rows. However, the front table was moved to the front of the classroom where the four teachers stood.

Mary stepped forward. "As you can see, the four of us are now wearing our uniforms to represent that we are part of this team. If you feel like you are a member of the team, you should too."

Harper didn't react, but several of the engineers mumbled and nodded.

"From now on Mr. Quinn will be teaching you, because he understands the lessons, and he also understands how you learn."

Mary, Sarara, and Kanara sat, while Quinn tapped the tablet he was holding, and the nanoboards lit up with the Moad ship design.

"Welcome everyone. Today's lesson is about what we know about the Moad technology. You can see the Ferris wheel they use to create artificial gravity…."

After that day, everyone but Harper wore the uniforms, and productivity skyrocketed. In the evenings, she and Quinn would work on the gravity-related devices.

Harper, unsurprisingly, took the longest time warming up to her, and Mary suspected that it was equally her fault and the general's. Even a week after the spaceship mishap, he was still sending her cold glares, but he hadn't said anything to her. In fact, he hadn't spoken a single word to her at all, but she wasn't complaining. She was glad about it, actually. He followed the orders laid out by her and Quinn, and that was all she needed from him. Soon enough, his glares stopped too.

Mary was sitting at her desk when there was a knock(ish) on the side of the tent.

"Dr. Goss. May I come in?"

It took Mary a second to recognize his voice. "Harper?"

"Yes," came the solemn reply.

Mary didn't know how to answer. She was curious why he was there, but did she want her mortal enemy in her tent? "Come in?"

Harper pushed aside the tent flap, leaving it open, and walked in wearing the new uniform. He didn't carry himself the same way she remembered. When she'd first arrived, he was tall and proud, but now he seemed humble.

Mary's eyes popped. "You're wearing your uniform."

"You said that when we feel like being a part of the team, we should wear it."

Mary smiled.

"I have been doing some thinking these past couple of weeks—some real, hard thinking."

Mary nodded, inviting him to sit and go on. He took the empty chair across from her desk, the one usually reserved for Quinn.

He took a deep breath. "I see now that I've been a real jerk to you. There, I said it."

Mary waited to see if there would be an actual apology.

"All this really puts things in perspective for me, and I see now that I didn't treat you the way I should have. I just saw you as a young upstart who thought you knew better than me, and I've always been the best in everything I do."

Mary could relate.

Harper sighed. "You challenged my way of thinking, and I guess I was just afraid that I was wrong, and I've never been wrong before. But I *was* wrong, and it almost cost me everything. I'm sorry."

Mary let the words stew in the air, taking them in and turning them over in her head. Finally, she nodded. "I can relate to that," she replied honestly. "I accept your apology, and I want to return it. I, too, have thought of how things have changed. How *I've* changed."

Harper seemed surprised at her words.

"Back when Sergeant Dow first recruited me, I thought if I worked hard enough, I would earn respect, but that was a misguided notion. I burned bridges with any man who I believed wasn't supporting me. I thought the whole world was against me—my professors, my classmates, even my peers—but I was really just working against myself."

They looked at each other for a moment.

"I have since learned that if I want respect, I have to give respect." She let out a bitter laugh. "It took two men almost blowing themselves up for me to realize all of this. How stupid is that?"

"I don't think it's stupid at all," Harper countered. "You saved my life after everything I did to make yours a nightmare." His eyes met hers, purpose shining in them as if he could will her to agree with him. "Now, moving on to the other reason why I came to see you...."

"What is it?" Mary asked, intrigued.

"I had a few ideas for a new ship design. I was hoping you would help me with it."

She smiled. "I would be happy to. Despite what happened, your X20 design showed real promise."

Harper rolled out the blueprints he was carrying.

Mary looked it over. "I'm impressed. You've incorporated human, Zalma, and what we know of Moad technology. Would you mind showing it to the class tomorrow, so we can all discuss it?"

Harper smiled and nodded.

One day, Mary was sitting in the mess hall, when Malcolm sat next to her.

"I heard you've been working with Harper on a new ship," was the first thing he said. "How's that been going?"

"Great, actually. Yeah—" she said as she saw his raised eyebrows, "I'm kind of surprised myself. He came to me the other day to apologize. We really cleared the air, then he asked for my help with the new ship design, and here we are."

Malcolm nodded and took a bite of his mashed potatoes. "And here we ar..." He was suddenly cut off by a shrieking wail and Mary nearly jumped out of her seat. It was coming from her pocket—more specifically, from her communicator. Around the room, every other communicator was going off in the same way, sounding like a cacophony of bells, sirens, and whistles.

"What's going on?" Mary asked Malcolm, who shrugged as he pulled out Benjamin. He looked lost, then turned his communicator to her. It read, "The Zalma deflectors have failed! Invasion imminent!"

# DID YOU ENJOY THIS BOOK?

Your feedback helps me provide the best quality books and helps other readers like you discover them.

It would mean the world to me if you took two minutes to share your thoughts about this book. You can leave a review with the retailer of your choice and/or send an email to *tony@tonybrichard.com* with your honest feedback.

Thank you, I really appreciate it.

# ACKNOWLEDGMENTS

Thank you to everyone who has helped this book become a reality. To my wife, Lydia, without whom this wouldn't be possible, to my Beta readers, to Lesia for designing the cover, to Carolin Petersen for editing and adding all of the final touches, and to every person who pitched in their ideas and opinions.

A special thanks to Gene Roddenberry, George Lucas, Dean Devlin, Roland Emmerich, Brad Wright, Jonathan Glassner, Ronald D. Moore, Ben Nedivi, Matt Wolpert, Greg Berlanti, and Todd Helbing for their wonderful creations (Star Trek, Star Wars, Stargate, For All Mankind, and Superman and Lois) that have and continue to inspire me.

# PRONUNCIATION GUIDE

| | |
|---|---|
| Ymit | YEM—it |
| Geogram | Ge—OG—ram |
| Agugua | A—GU—gwa |
| Joanua | Jo—ANN—wa |
| Edugra | Ed—OOO—gra |
| Sarara | Sa—RAR—ah |
| Kanara | Kan—ARR—ah |
| Zalma | ZALL—mah |
| Zalmen | ZALL—men |
| Moad | Moe—ADD |
| Moadites | Moe—ADytes |

# SERIES TIMELINE

### ROSWELL: FIRST CONTACT
*Malcolm Dow & Adam Rabinowitz: Episode 1*

### NEGOTIATIONS
*Ryan Wilcox: Episode 1*

### THE GOOD, THE BAD, AND THE UNDECIDED
*Greg Newman: Episode 1*

### DEFYING GRAVITY
*Mary Goss: Episode 1*

*(spanning the entire timeline)*

### CHARLIE'S BIG CHANCE
*Charlie Baker: Episode 1*

### THE WOUNDLESS WAR
*Frank Jones: Episode 1*

### FROM ROSWELL TO AREA 51: THE NOVEL
*(a single "cinematic cut" that braids all six POVs in chronological order)*

Earth's Secret Alliance is a series of clean,
family friendly, uplifting,
one-to-two-hour short stories.

## ROSWELL: FIRST CONTACT

When Private Malcolm Dow went to clean up a crashed weather balloon, hey came face-to-face with an alien instead.

Adam Rabinowitz was one of those wimps who followed Dow around, hoping for protection from the bullies.

While Dow was reluctant, Rabinowitz instantly took on the Alien's plight – military help for his besieged planet, Zalma. But when he gets caught, it's up to Dow to save the day.

If they fail, it's not just Zalma; Earth may be captured or destroyed next. But if they are to succeed, they must work around the chain of command to avoid the anti-alien majority.

## NEGOTIATIONS

The Zalmen have arrived on Earth hungry for collaboration. But they're about to lose their appetite.

In 1947, a peaceful day at home for talented negotiator Ryan Wilcox is rudely interrupted by a phone call from the president. With the help of General Jones and Malcolm Dow, he's to arrange an interplanetary alliance. It's an opportunity that Earth can't afford to miss. The aliens offer knowledge that will speed up the Human advance by hundreds of years.

But as with any friendship, the beginning stages require a delicate approach. And there's one issue of "delicacy" that threatens to turn their partnership into an outright war.

Will Ryan the wordsmith rise to the challenge and find common ground? Or is it the end of life as we know it?

## THE GOOD, THE BAD, AND THE UNDECIDED

Major General Greg Newman has always been self-centered and opportunistic-even using WWII as a stepping stone to advance his career. Now that the war is over, he's looking for a new way to add more stars to his shoulders. Soon Greg is approached about a secret mission spying on a superior officer and a classified research facility. He hopes this job will land him that quick promotion but has reservations about surveilling this officer. Voicing his concern is only met with not-so-subtle threats.

Now entangled in a diabolical plan, Greg questions which boundaries he's unwilling to cross. If he doesn't jettison his morals entirely, then his career will surely go down in flames. Greg must decide who to trust, and that becomes a choice between a quick promotion, or saving his country—and maybe even the world.

CHARLIE'S BIG CHANCE

Aliens. A notebook. A secret no one will believe.

Charlie Baker is 12 years old, dreams of being a reporter, and uses a wheel-chair to get around her small town. When she stumbles across a crashed alien ship near Roswell, everything changes.

Now Charlie has a chance to write the story of a lifetime—but telling the truth might put the aliens in danger. Can she keep their secret, even as the military closes in?

THE WOUNDLESS WAR

In 1947, a UFO crash-lands in Roswell, New Mexico, bringing General Frank Jones face to face with the alien Zalmen. Desperate for help, the Zalmen reveal their advanced technology, but with a catch: they are pacifists, and will only allow Frank to use it if he doesn't kill anyone. As the clock ticks down and the enemy Moad close in, Frank must find a way to save the Zalmen and their planet without taking any lives. But if he fails, the Moad will use the Zalmen's technology against Earth, with devastating consequences.

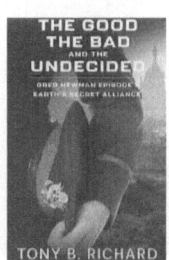

# ABOUT THE AUTHOR

Tony B. Richard lives in Langley, British Columbia.
He is a computer programmer (coder) and instructor.
This grand adventure has been in his head for decades,
and during the Covid-19 pandemic, he thought it was
finally time to put it down on paper.

*"Differences are something to be celebrated, not feared."*
—TONY B. RICHARD

YOU CAN CONTACT HIM WITH QUESTIONS OR
COMMENTS AT:

*Website: www.tonybrichard.com*
*Email: tony@tonybrichard.com*
*Facebook: EarthsSecretAlliance*
*Twitter: @TonyBRichard1*
*Instagram: tony_b_richard*
*Goodreads: Tony B. Richard*

www.ingramcontent.com/pod-product-compliance
Lightning Source LLC
Chambersburg PA
CBHW030537130626
46552CB00006B/2299